"You're hurting,

Micah kneeled before arms.

"I'm fine," Landy insisted, holding herself away from him, hoping to stave off the warmth that emanated from his body along with the fresh scent of soap.

"Ms. Wisdom." He looked down into her face. "I am trying my best to use manners my mama taught me. The least you can do is go along with it and maybe I won't drop you."

She relaxed in spite of herself. "Your mama would be proud."

"I hope so." He opened the car door, propped his foot on the inside running board so that her backside rested on his thigh...and kissed her.

Oh, yes, was all she had time to think before her senses took over. The age-old dance was slow and warm and tasted sweet.

"That wasn't part of what my mama taught me," he said when the kiss ended.

Dear Reader,

In a town near where we live, a paved walkway meanders along the Wabash River. The path is well-lit and has benches and the occasional swing for the weary. My husband and I walk there when the weather permits, talking about our days, about the kids and grandkids, saying "remember when" and finishing each other's sentences the way long-married people tend to do.

The writer in me also says "what if" on those treks, and that's where the story of *The Debutante's Second Chance* was born. "What if," I asked my husband, "there was an underground railroad that no one knew about, where battered wives and abused children found safety? And what if..."

He liked the idea. I hope you do, too.

Liz Flaherty

THE DEBUTANTE'S SECOND CHANCE

LIZ FLAHERTY

SPECIAL EDITION

Published by Silhouette Books

America's Publisher of Contemporary Romance

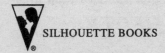

SILHOUETTE BOOKS

ISBN-13: 978-0-373-24854-4
ISBN-10:   0-373-24854-7

THE DEBUTANTE'S SECOND CHANCE

Copyright © 2007 by Liz Flaherty

Books by Liz Flaherty

Silhouette Special Edition

The Debutante's Second Chance #1854

LIZ FLAHERTY

When Liz Flaherty was eleven, she read *Little Women* until the covers literally fell off. She learned about the 1800s and love and deliverance and the purity of joy and she thought, Wow, this is what I want to do when I grow up.

By the time she was twenty-three, she was married with three children under four and a three-bedroom-ranch in a subdivision. Late at night, exhausted, she sat in the corner of the couch and read romance novels and learned about foreign countries and love and deliverance and the purity of joy and she thought, Hmmm, I could do that. Later.

In her 30s, with the three children in their teens and an old farmhouse in the country, she sat on the bleachers and read more romance novels and learned about the empowerment of women and love and deliverance and the purity of joy and thought, Yes! Soon!

Er, several years later, Liz still has the same three children, along with the spouses and grandchildren they've gifted her with, the same husband and the same old farmhouse. She still reads romance and believes in love and deliverance and the purity of joy. And, not that she's grown up yet, but Later and Soon have arrived and *The Debutante's Second Chance* is the result.

Liz loves to hear from readers and can be reached at lizkflaherty@yahoo.com.

For Tahne Flaherty, Kari Wilson, Laura Flaherty,
Chris Flaherty, Jim Wilson and Jeremy Flaherty.
Some by blood and some in-law,
but all the children of my heart.

Prologue

Window Over the Sink, Taft Tribune: *Allow me to introduce myself. My name is Susan, I'm married to my high-school heartthrob, and have three great kids. I named this column "Window Over the Sink" because it's my favorite part of my house. I call it the poor woman's therapist, because when I look through its panes at the Twilight River and imagine the breeze singing through the sycamores and maples and cotton- woods, I feel immense comfort. I'm writing this first column right around April Fool's day because that's something else that gives comfort in this life: being a damn fool once in a while....*

The first column appeared on Micah Walker's desk on the last day of March, before he'd even put out the first issue of the *Taft Tribune* with his name on the masthead as the owner-editor. The article was in a plain, white, number-ten envelope that had been mailed in Taft; the return address was a post office box. The column ran about seven hundred words, neatly printed on a laser printer. Some of it, like "high-school heartthrob," made his journalistic side wince, but the terminology fit in the small Indiana town on the Twilight River. If he tightened it a little, it would fit right into the *Tribune*.

Allison Scott, the reporter who had come with him from Lexington to work on the *Tribune*, stood in the doorway of his office. "Did you write this by any chance?" he asked when she came in. He handed her the column.

"No," she said instantly, and began to read. When she was finished, she looked wistful. "I kind of wish I had. It's not technically perfect, but you sure can feel it."

"You're a romantic." She was, but that didn't stop her from being one of the finest reporters he'd ever met. "I'll tighten it up and run it. I don't think 'Susan Billings' is her real name, but that's who we'll make the check out to."

"Don't tighten it," Allie suggested. "Let the feelings come through." She turned to go.

He nodded. "Where are you off to?"

"A meeting. Domestic Violence Awareness. They're going to discuss a sheltering system for battered women and children, the Safe Harbor Railroad."

Micah shook his head. "Little towns are supposed to

be utopian. They shouldn't need that kind of group. Let me know if there's something the paper can do," he said, "without endangering anyone, I mean."

"I don't know if they'll even let me in. Secrecy is the reason for its success, I guess."

He nodded, half-listening. "How's your mother?" he asked, without looking up.

"What?" Allie sounded startled.

"You know, your mom. How's she doing?" Micah never interfered in anyone's private life; he was pretty proud of remembering that Allie's mother had been ill.

"Oh. Better. Much better." But she seemed shaken by the question.

"Good." He smiled absently in her direction, his mind already moving away. "That's good."

"Well."

She seemed uncharacteristically indecisive, and he looked at her again. "Was there something else, Allie? Do you need a few more days off?"

"No. No, thanks." She straightened. "Well, I'm off to the meeting. You're right, though—how could a place that produces a 'Window Over the Sink' need an Underground Railroad? It just seems wrong."

Chapter One

Window Over the Sink, Taft Tribune: *Sometimes I miss having heroes. All the ones I knew when I was young seem to have developed feet of clay and leapt without conscience from the pedestals I placed them on. But today I lay on an uncomfortable cot and gave blood. I looked around at the people who gave their time freely, at the others who gave their blood just as freely. I saw a minister, a newspaper editor, a registered nurse who was spending her day off inserting slender needles into veins, half the Taft High School baseball team still wearing their practice jerseys. And I realized there are heroes all around*

us, and they don't need to be on pedestals because
they don't have time for that kind of nonsense.

Landy Wisdom didn't look at all the way Micah remembered her from high school. Her hair had been the
color of sunlight then, her eyes like the darkest of the
lilacs that grew in studied profusion in her grandmother's side yard. Her figure had been lithe and nubile
in her designer jeans and silk blouses and cashmere
blazers. Her clothes hadn't been bought at JC Penney or
Kmart like most everyone else's, but on shopping trips
to Cincinnati and Louisville. She'd been, in a town
without a social scale, a debutante. Her grandmother had
owned the brewery and was one of the few people in
town who had servants. Landy's boyfriend had been the
high school quarterback, the son of Taft's best-known
attorney, who'd gone on to stardom at Notre Dame.

But there had been more to Landy than that. Her best
friend had been Jessie Titus, whose grandmother had
kept house for old Mrs. Wisdom. Landy had aided with
her grandmother's charities, but she'd been hands-on
help. She'd washed dishes at dinners, cleaned up after
dances and walked every inch of every walkathon ever
held in Taft.

Micah remembered talking to her once as she
slogged through rain for crippled children. She hadn't
had a raincoat because she'd tossed it over the shoulders of the minister's wife, and mud splashed up her
legs as she walked.

"Who *are* you?" he'd demanded. He'd been so angry

then, furious at the "haves" in what he was finding to be a "have-not" world. The fact that Landy Wisdom didn't fit into his idea of a "have" made him even angrier. People who had it all didn't share things when that sharing got them wet, cold and muddy.

"I'm just Landy," she'd said quietly, a hurt look in her eyes, "and I'm sorry you don't like me."

Twenty years later, standing in line in his London Fog raincoat and watching Landis Wisdom as she wrote down information for the Red Cross blood bank, Micah felt a niggle of shame because he'd put that look in her eyes. Good writing and solid investments had made him into one of the "haves" he'd so despised, and along with the money had come the realization that there really wasn't that much difference in people.

But he still wondered who she really was, and what had happened to the debutante he remembered. The hair color had deepened to the hue of honey, the eyes to violet. She wore a navy blue sweater with faded jeans and no makeup, no jewelry other than tiny pearls in her ears, not even polish on what appeared to be chewed-to-the-quick fingernails. Her figure had thickened a little over the years, but not much. She still looked nice.

But not like a debutante. Not like the richest girl in town. She'd evidently not jumped on the plastic surgery bandwagon, because small lines had carved themselves into the skin at the corners of her eyes, at the outer edges of her mouth, in her forehead between her eyebrows. She looked every minute of her thirty-six years.

"Are you a first-time donor?"

He realized with a start that the husky voice he heard was hers and that she was speaking to him.

"First time here," he said, suddenly remembering why he was in the basement of the Taft United Methodist Church. "I just moved here two weeks ago, but I have a Red Cross card somewhere." He rummaged in his wallet, feeling as clumsy and foolish as he had on that walkathon.

"Well, I'll be damned." Another voice, softer and filled with laughter, made him look for its source. "Look up, Landy, and see who you're waiting on."

"Don't swear in church, Jess. Our grandmothers will come back and haunt us." But Landy looked up, and Micah saw recognition leap into her eyes. They were like pansies, not violets. Dark and mysterious and tragic.

"Micah Walker." She sounded glad to see him, and the welcome in her voice opened up a warm place inside him, a place he wasn't about to look into. "I heard you and your dad moved back. You bought the *Tribune?*"

He nodded, and Jessie said, "About time someone bought that rag. Maybe you can turn it into a real newspaper."

Her voice made Micah remember she was there, standing beside Landy's chair, and he extended his hand. "Jessie, it's good to see you." Her name tag said "Jessie Brown" and he remembered that she was a widow.

"Micah, is that your card?" Landy asked. "I'd love to talk to you, but there's someone waiting."

"Oh, sorry." Micah turned to apologize to the person behind him, recognized his father and grinned instead before returning his attention to Landy. "It's all right, it's just some old coot."

She grinned back at him, the expression having more of an effect on him than Ethan's thump between his shoulder blades. He thought abstractedly that the debutante wasn't entirely gone; Landy's front teeth were beautifully but undeniably capped.

After Jessie had taken a pint of his blood, the volunteers in the church kitchen gave him a ham salad sandwich and a glass of juice. "Wait over there a bit," she'd said, "till you get your legs back."

He exchanged pleasantries with the volunteers, recognizing Mrs. Burnside, his high school geometry teacher, among them. Another donor passed behind him and sat at the end of the table, muttering thanks to Mrs. Burnside when she brought him his sandwich and drink.

Micah continued talking to the woman on his right, whose name was Jenny and who owned the café downtown, appropriately named Down at Jenny's. But he felt the hair on the back of his neck standing on end and knew he was being stared at. He looked toward Landy's table, but she was busy. In profile, her face looked pale, and he saw that the hands that shuffled the papers on the table were shaking. Frowning, he looked toward the end of the table.

Lucas Trent hadn't changed much in twenty years. He was bigger, his florid complexion redder, but he was still handsome, wearing the patina of the city as surely as he did his expensive suit. Micah wondered, not for the first time, what had kept Trent in Taft when he obviously held the two-stoplight town in the lowest kind of contempt.

The attorney used to stand at the fence at football games. "Come on, you dumb farm boys," he'd shout. "Protect your quarterback." The quarterback, of course, being Blake Trent, Landy's boyfriend and Lucas's son.

"Mr. Trent." Micah nodded a polite greeting.

"Walker." Trent returned the nod. "Heard you were back in town. Do you plan on staying long?"

"Yes, sir. I've bought the *Taft Tribune*."

"Made a success of yourself, have you." It wasn't a question, and Trent's expression was cold and dark. "Next thing we know, you'll buy a house on River Walk and start socializing with my erstwhile daughter-in-law."

"Erstwhile?" That wasn't a word used much in places like Taft. Most people would have said *ex-daughter-in-law* or *son's former wife*.

The simplicity of speech had been only one of the things about Taft he'd been happy to leave. He'd found the town stifling as a teenager and had been happy to shake its river valley dust from his feet when he went away to college. Graduation had landed him a job in Lexington, Kentucky, and he'd loved it there.

"You mean you haven't caught up with the gossip yet?" Trent's face was drawn and angry, the kind of anger that comes with suffering. "No hint of scandal has passed under your journalistic nose?"

Micah shifted impatiently in his chair, wondering what was taking his father so long. "I try not to deal in scandal unless it involves hard news."

"Oh, it was hard all night." The attorney shuddered, and pain crossed his face. "Blake's dead," Trent said, "and Landis is the reason why."

Landy helped put the church basement in order, trying not to watch the tableau across the room. Even so, she saw Micah's face harden and knew Lucas had told him.

Micah would believe whatever Lucas said. He'd never liked her anyway, would be eager to accept that she was not only a poor little rich girl but a murderer as well.

"Landy." Mrs. Burnside's voice reached her. "Would you help me in here, dear?"

"In here" was the kitchen. She'd have to walk past the table where Micah sat with his father and Lucas Trent and feel their baleful gazes burning holes into the back of her sweater. She wondered why it was the unhappy things, like painful memories and people thinking badly of you and the need for donated blood, that seemed to be unending. Happy spaces in time were always fleeting.

"Don't slump." Jessie's voice came softly. She stood beside Landy, pulling on her coat. "Stand tall and smile like there's nothing that could ever reach you. Don't make me whack your spine to straighten you up the way Grandma used to."

Landy stretched up tall just the way Evelyn Titus had taught her. "See you later, Jess. Kiss the kids for me." She drew her mouth into a smile and moved across the room, going to the sink to dry the pitchers used for juice.

"Good turnout today," said Mrs. Burnside.

Landy nodded, trying to think of something to say. "So, how do you like being retired, Mrs. Burnside?"

"You can call me Nancy, dear. We're not in geometry class anymore. Retirement's all right. I miss the kids, especially those few every year who soaked up information like a sponge." She tilted her head and lowered her voice. "Like that Walker boy. He wasn't gifted, or even extraordinarily intelligent, but he loved learning as much as anyone I ever taught. He had a bad reputation, but he was a pleasure to have in class."

"Was he?" Micah had been in Blake's class, two years ahead of Landy. He'd seemed taciturn and always angry. Blake hadn't liked him, so she'd avoided him. Even then, it was better not to cross Blake.

Lucas brought his glass and plate to where they stood. "Better be careful, Nancy," he warned, "who you let in here. There's no telling what's in their blood."

"Go back to your office, Lucas." Her voice was frosty. "We don't have time for this."

Landy looked past her former father-in-law at where Micah still sat at the table. He was watching, his gray eyes expressionless. He spoke to his father in a low murmur, but his gaze never left the scene at the sink.

"Landy." Micah's voice was still quiet, but it carried easily to where she stood. "Jenny said you were a Realtor. Could you show me some houses? The bed and breakfast is comfortable, but I need something permanent."

Landy almost grinned. She was, indeed, a licensed Realtor, but her sole contribution to the field was answering the phones at Davis Realty when the receptionist didn't show up for work.

"Of course," she said, and some devil made her add, "Any particular area?"

He got to his feet, reaching for his coat. "Yeah, I was thinking about something on the River Walk."

He hadn't been thinking that at all, but it was worth the lie to see the look of dismay on Lucas Trent's face, the quick shimmer of glee that crossed Landy's features. "Are you free now?" Micah asked. "I could buy you a cup of coffee and give you an idea what I'm looking for."

Mrs. Burnside took the pitcher Landy was drying from her hands. "She's free, but you buy her some dinner, too, Micah. She doesn't eat enough to keep a bird alive."

"You kids go ahead." Micah's father spoke. "I'll help finish up here."

Landy looked as though she wanted to argue, but Nancy Burnside was holding out her black pea coat expectantly. "All right," Landy said finally, slipping her arms into the extended sleeves.

Micah put a hand under her elbow as they ascended the basement stairs. She had a hitch in her walk, and he wondered if she was on the tail end of a sprained ankle.

He didn't ask, but when she pitched slightly sideways at the landing, he tightened his hand.

"I really don't do much with real estate," she said. "Taking the course was just one of the things I did to keep busy at a time in my life."

"I know you don't." Jenny had told him that much.

They crossed the church foyer, and he kept his hand under her arm, liking its warmth, the way the heat moved through his own veins.

In a few minutes, they were seated across from each other in the back booth of the café, Jenny's fresh coffee steaming between them.

"What kind of house do you have in mind?" asked Landy.

"Old. Big. Near the river."

"Sort of 'in your face?'"

"Not really, although I'm sure the Lucas Trents in town will take it as such." He shrugged. "I can't help that."

"Tell me about you," she urged, lifting her cup to her mouth. "What have you done with your life?"

Her hands weren't like he remembered them, either, not that he'd paid that much attention to them twenty years ago; her other parts had been much more interesting. In addition to the short, unpolished nails and the fingers' lack of rings, the hands were thin and capable-looking. A few of the knuckles were more prominent than the others, one of the little fingers crooked. She didn't flutter her hands or fidget with them the way nervous people he knew did; nevertheless, he felt tension emanating from her.

"I went to college," he said, "at the University of Kentucky and stayed in Lexington after that as a reporter and a columnist. I loved what I did, even though it didn't leave a whole lot of time for a normal life. Then a year and a half ago, my mom died. My dad was lost without her, and the only time he ever showed any interest in anything was when we talked about Taft. The paper was for sale, so here we are."

"It's nice to have you back," she said politely. "Do you want to look at some houses now? I can pick up keys and take you to ones that are empty. I'm afraid I don't know what's available, but we can look at the listings."

Micah wanted to touch her pale cheek, wanted to murmur, "It's all right. Nothing can hurt you now," and convince her the words were true. He kept his hands wrapped around his cup.

"At least with this rain, you'll be seeing the properties at their worst, so there won't be any unpleasant surprises later." Her tone was businesslike and crisp, and her eyes avoided his.

"Fine," he said quietly. "Let's look."

Narrow and tortuous, the Twilight River flowed slow and lackadaisical between wooded hills and dumped itself unceremoniously into the Ohio. Just before reaching the Ohio, the Twilight widened and splattered, looking on the map like nothing so much as a human fist with a short, extended thumb. Taft nestled in the V between the thumb and the fist, beginning toward the end of its second hundred years to meander around the edge of the curled fingers of the river.

Some of Taft's earliest inhabitants—the richer ones—had made a walkway around the thumb, complete with a narrow bridge that spanned the appendage. The corridor's cobblestones had been carefully maintained over the years, its gaslights eventually replaced by electricity, and its park benches painted green each year and replaced as needed. The walkway was low enough to have been flooded a few times, but high enough to elude most of Mother Nature's watery tantrums.

Houses surrounded the walkway on oddly shaped lots, scarcely visible even to each other when trees were in full leaf. Most of the houses were old, some of them large and elegant, some small and cozy.

Landy had grown up here, in her grandmother's house at the end of the thumb. Blake Trent had lived four houses away, Jessie Titus in Landy's grandmother's carriage house.

Micah had lived across town in what was optimistically termed a subdivision. Three bedroom, one bath ranch houses, six to the acre, filled the neighborhood. A sign at its entrance told all comers its name was Twilight View, but everyone knew it as the Bowery.

"Do you live in your grandmother's house?" asked Micah, driving slowly up the wide avenue the houses faced.

"I sold it after…Blake died. The church bought it for a parsonage. I was going to start over somewhere else, but I didn't really want to leave Taft." She gestured toward the end of the thumb. "My house is further down."

Micah turned into the driveway of the house that was for sale, and he saw out of the corner of his eye that she was smiling.

"This is my favorite house on River Walk," she said, unfastening her seat belt before he'd even stopped the car. "It's where Eli St. John grew up. Remember him?"

Who could forget Eli? Class president. Another of the running backs from the high school football team. He'd been neither as flamboyant as Blake nor as good as Micah. "I am known," he had said from his spot as the sixth man on the basketball team, "as the deuce of all trades because I'm not good enough to be a jack, much less a master." He'd been, if guys had talked about things like that, Micah's best friend.

Eli, would you come and visit if I lived in your old house?

Micah felt a surge of pleasure with the memories, and—annoyed with himself for the pleasure—said gruffly, "Is he still in Taft?"

Landy nodded. "Not still, but again, like you. He got divorced a few years ago and came back here to raise his kids."

"What does he do?" Without waiting for an answer, he got out of the car and walked around to open her door, but she was already out, closing the door herself.

"He's the min—"

She was interrupted by a shout. "Well, it is him. I thought for sure you were making it up, Landy."

Micah felt his shoulders being thumped and turned to look into Eli St. John's open countenance. The face had changed so little since he'd last seen it that Micah thought for a disjointed moment that Eli was still eighteen.

"Micah, it's so good to see you."

"Eli." Micah did a little thumping of his own, and felt his throat tighten.

"Landy called and told me you were coming to look at the folks' house," said Eli, leading the way to the front door, "so I came over to hide where the roof is leaking and stop up all the gushers coming into the basement."

Standing in the foyer of the St. John house, with his coat dripping onto the hardwood floor, Micah felt as though he never wanted to leave it. He hadn't been inside it for twenty years, but he remembered where the fireplace would be, flanked by built-in bookcases with glass doors. He knew the floor of the living room would be constructed of wide planks, with the imperfections and irregularities of age adding to its beauty. He knew, before he peered into the library or the formal dining room or the family room off the kitchen, before he walked up the curving front stair-case or the crooked, narrow back one, that he'd come home.

Halfway up the front stairs, he said, "I'll take it."

Eli, following him, stopped. "You wouldn't like to know how much it is?"

He shrugged. "Are you going to screw me?"

"No."

Micah gave him a sideways grin. "Then, no, I don't need to know right now. When can I move in?"

"Tomorrow."

He met Eli's outstretched hand with his own. "Tomorrow? For all you know, I'm a con man looking for a respectable place to launder money."

Eli's smile was enigmatic. "I was on the football field with you. I know better. Landis, you going to take care of this?"

Micah had forgotten she was there, so enthralled had he been by the house. He looked down at where she stood, his gaze meeting hers in mute apology. But she was laughing, and her eyes were sparkling.

How could he, for even one minute, have forgotten her presence?

"Couldn't you two at least talk this out a little more so I will have earned my commission?"

Eli looked at his watch. "I don't have time. I have to make sure the madding crowd over there doesn't dismantle the dining room, and then I have to make myself look properly preacherly before the evening service. Call me in the morning, Micah, and we'll finish this over breakfast."

He wrung Micah's hand again, sketched a wave to Landy as he passed her, and was gone.

"Preacherly?" said Micah.

"Eli's the minister at the Methodist Church."

"A minister?" But it fit, Micah realized after a moment—Eli was one of the good guys.

His attention shifted back to Landy. "You never did have anything to eat," he said suddenly. "Let me buy you dinner."

Chapter Two

Window Over the Sink, Taft Tribune: *April is such a beautiful month. Things start getting green again and there's hope everywhere and baseball fields ring with the sounds of joy.*

But you have to watch for storms in April, have to listen to tornado warnings and watches and open your basement door and keep a bottle of water and a first-aid kit down there in case something bad happens. Sometimes the price we pay for spring is a heavy one.

The fact that she wanted to have dinner with Micah surprised Landy. She hadn't shared a meal alone with a man since the last time with Blake. Her husband had skimmed his meat across the table like a pebble on a pond and she'd said, "I'm sorry," even though there had been nothing wrong with the pork chop—everything was wrong with the marriage, where terror and abuse had places at the dinner table.

She hesitated, lost in memory, and was brought back to the present by Micah's questioning gaze. "All right," she said, "but come to my house. My cooking is the best example of mediocrity you'll find this side of a fast-food place. But I have some chili I can heat up that'll be perfect for a rainy night like this. We can get there in two minutes on the Walk." And it was safe. Nothing could happen to her there in a house where Blake had never been, where pain had never lived.

Micah nodded, a smile coming into his eyes. She locked the St. John house and handed him the key, and he pocketed it without comment. She realized that houses didn't mean the same thing to men that they did to women. Men seemed to see them as investments, mere buildings to keep them out of the rain, while women saw them as safe havens, warmth against the cold and extensions of themselves. They wanted the decor to reflect their personalities and be welcoming; men wanted it to be cheap and not show dirt.

"What are your plans for the paper?" she asked. "It's become so political in recent years. Are you going to keep it that way?"

"No."

He took her arm, and she knew he'd noticed her limp. People always did.

"Remember when we were kids?" he asked. "The news was mostly local. Weddings, funerals, fiftieth anniversary parties. The columnists, even the political ones, wrote from the slant of living in a little river town. Kind of like the towns Tom Bodett and Garrison Keillor write about."

"I remember. Everyone in town took the paper then."

"Right. And if a paper boy or girl forgot to deliver it, the editor took a copy out to the subscriber the same night and gave him the next week free."

They were at her back steps now, and she tried not to lean on his arm as they walked up. Her leg wasn't more painful when she climbed stairs, but lifting her foot repeatedly was awkward and tiring.

"Is that what you're going to do? Bring that back?" *Keep him talking and he won't ask you why you limp.*

"I'm going to try to," he corrected her. "It was that kind of newspaper that made me want to be a journalist."

She led the way into the kitchen of her house, tossing her coat over the back of a chair to dry. "Let me take your coat."

She hung his raincoat in the laundry room and returned to find him standing at the cold fireplace in the kitchen. "Light a fire if you'd like," she suggested. "I know it's not that cold, but the chill from the rain gets into your bones." *Especially ones that have been broken.* She longed to swallow some aspirin to ease the ache in her leg, but didn't want to invite comment.

He knelt before the fireplace, laying a fire carefully. "Was this kitchen like this when you moved in?"

"Pretty much, though I refinished the old floor and put up wallpaper everywhere. Sam down at the paint store goes into ecstasy when he sees me coming. I'm pretty sure I'm putting his oldest daughter through medical school." She turned a burner on low under a pot of chili and went to the windows that overlooked the river, turning the wands that closed the blinds. "Do you want to see the rest of the house?" She couldn't keep the pride out of her voice.

"Sure." He straightened and looked around. "I'd like for the St. John house to feel like this one. Cozy, I guess, but not lacy or fussy."

She grinned at him. "The lace and fuss are upstairs. Come on."

Micah was a perfect house tourist; he liked everything, even the rose-strewn wallpaper in her bedroom and bathroom.

"Did you have a decorator?" he asked.

"I did it myself," she said. "Well, me and Sam and Jessie and everyone I hired to do the things I was afraid I'd screw up."

They sat at the kitchen table with their dinner. "Blake had a designer do Grandmother's house when we moved into it," she said, "and it was beautiful, but Jessie said it felt like a hotel she couldn't afford to stay in."

Landy watched Micah covertly while they ate, putting bits and pieces of what she saw into the safe place where she kept good memories.

He was tall and broad-shouldered like her husband had been, but had maintained his muscled build in a way that Blake had not. Micah's dark brown hair was well cut, but not particularly neat, looking as though he combed it with his fingers throughout the day. He squinted sometimes, and she pictured his lean face with reading glasses sliding down his nose. His eyes were the same gray as the pewter pitcher on the mantel, fringed by thick lashes. His smile was wide and lovely, and came seldom. His hand, when he'd held her arm, had been strong but not bruising. She didn't think Micah Walker had a need to convey power; it was there in his quiet presence.

Without in the least meaning to, Landy sighed.

Across the fat candles that flickered between them, Micah caught and held her gaze. "What happened?" he asked, and she knew he wasn't asking her about the sigh.

She hesitated. He was a reporter, she reminded herself. He was like those people who had dogged her every step for days, had been at the hospital, the mortuary, in the courtroom and camped in the front and back yards of Grandmother's house. They had held microphones in her face and shouted questions at her. They had created an obstacle course that a woman on crutches could scarcely navigate.

But the one time she had fallen, when, blinded by tears, she had tripped over someone's thick black cord, one of the reporters had stuffed her recorder into her pocket and come to Landy's aid. She had helped her up the steps and into the house, speaking quietly in her ear. The voice had been low, but the words had included the term "predatory sons of bitches" and Landy had laughed in spite of everything. The young woman helped her to a seat and then left her alone, and when Landy got up and peered outside through a lifted corner of a curtain, there had been no one left in her yard.

She'd always wanted to thank the reporter for rescuing her, but had never seen her again in the hordes who had followed her until someone else's drama took news media precedence over hers.

"You were the debutante," said Micah. "Your life was supposed to be charmed." His voice was soft, gentle, the kind of voice that could lull you into thinking you were safe. Could, if the time was right, talk you into bed naked before you knew your bra was unfastened.

"I never knew what I did," she said, "to make you think I was like that. I went to the same school, church, Kmart that everyone else did, but I couldn't ever be just everyone else. To you, anyway."

"I know," he said. "When I was eighteen, I divided the world into those who had and those who didn't. You had, which made you worthy of my contempt. At the time, I imagine I thought your family even hired people to go to the bathroom for you."

The self-directed sarcasm startled a laugh from her. "Not quite," she said, "but speaking of bathrooms, would you excuse me?"

In the pretty little powder room under the stairs, she swallowed three extra-strength pain relievers and willed them to work. The ache in her leg had become a raging fire, with little arrows of flame shooting and swirling all the way from her hip to her ankle.

They sat in comfortable chairs in front of the fireplace, their coffee on a cloth-covered round table between them. Landy stretched her jeans-clad legs out straight, propping her feet on the ottoman the chairs shared, and Micah saw a spasm of pain cross her face. The expression cleared immediately, however, to be replaced with a Mona Lisa smile he recognized as a mask.

"It's pretty much a classic story," she said. "Blake started hitting me in high school, stopped while we were in college, and started up again before we'd been married three months. We'd go to counseling, it would get better, then he'd drink and it would happen again. It became such a cycle I was almost able to mark it on a calendar."

She spoke without expression, though the color in the cheek he could see was hectic and her hands had that look about them again. That tension that made her grip her coffee cup and raise it to her lips in a studied motion.

"Why?" He had to force the word out.

"Why what? Why did an intelligent woman stay with an abusive husband? I told you it was a classic story—my reasons are just as classic. He didn't mean to, I deserved it, it won't happen again, I can't manage on my own because I don't know how. You've probably heard them all before."

He nodded slightly, his jaw hurting from being clamped so tightly. *This shouldn't have happened to her. It shouldn't happen to anyone, but especially her. She's fragile, small, a debutante, for God's sake.*

"Finally, five years ago, we got divorced. It was very civilized, as divorces go. I kept Grandmother's house and Blake married his secretary and went to a law firm in Indianapolis. It was more prestigious than his father's firm. Also less accepting of his lax professional standards. He was back with his father within a year."

She rose, straightening slowly, and limped to the coffeepot, bringing it back and refilling their cups. When she returned to her seat, she gave a small gasp and grasped her leg. "Charley horse," she said, with a hitching little laugh.

He nodded, knowing she lied. He wanted to offer to rub the pain from her leg, but sensed the gesture wouldn't be welcome.

"Blake's new wife came to my house late one night two and a half years ago. It was storming to beat the band and she asked for shelter. I remember thinking how much smarter she was than I'd been, getting away earlier instead of waiting for him to change. Blake arrived within the hour."

Micah wanted to tell her to stop. The fact that his jaw hurt and her leg hurt and the fire needed another log were all good reasons for her to stop, weren't they?

She set down her cup, and he saw that the hand with the chewed fingernails and bumpy knuckles trembled the way it had that afternoon in the church basement. He took it in his and held it, not saying anything.

"She and I were at the top of the stairs when he let himself in—I'd never changed the locks, since the divorce was so civilized. What an idiot I was." She shuddered, and her fingers tightened around his. "But it was different this time, because Blake had a gun. I'd felt so powerful, so alive, after we were divorced that apparently I thought I could stop bullets, because I stepped in front of his wife. But he wasn't interested in me and tried to push me out of the way. I grabbed his arm—can you believe that? The man had a gun and I *grabbed his arm.* I knocked him off balance and when he went down the stairs, he took me with him."

She swallowed hard, and her eyes were dark and sad, glimmering with unshed tears. "The gun went off, just like in the movies. God, what a horrendous noise that makes. I had blood all over me and I was hurt, so I thought I'd been shot, but when I turned my head, he was lying there and not moving. He died on the way to the hospital."

"Did his wife tell a different story?"

"No, but Lucas didn't believe either one of us." She rubbed her leg with her free hand, not looking at him. "I kept remembering how much I'd loved Blake, how much fun he could be when he wanted to. I thought of how he insisted I learn to use a gun correctly to keep me safe. It's easy to blame yourself when the other person is dead."

"What happened then?"

"Lucas lost the case, I sold Grandmother's house to the church and life went on. On the surface, at least. Underneath—" she hesitated and drew her hand from his "—underneath, I think my life ended when Blake's did."

He gestured toward her leg. "Is that a leftover from the fall down the stairs?"

She nodded. "It was broken in three places. The surgeon wants to operate again, but I keep putting it off."

Micah lifted his hand to her face, cupping her cheek and stroking a tear from her lashes with his thumb. "I think maybe your life's broken, like your leg was, but not over. Some healing takes a long time."

She nodded. "But some things never heal at all."

Chapter Three

Window Over the Sink, Taft Tribune: *Don't you just hate moving? On Susan's personal list of favorites, it's right up there with root canal and cleaning the mold out of the refrigerator. But there's an upside to it. When you're actually living in your new home, sleeping in your own bed, and spilling grape juice on your own new carpet, you get a different feeling from any other. You feel at home—there's nothing any better than that. Sometimes, moving is a second, third, or last chance at a brave, wonderful new life.*

Landy helped Micah move into the St. John house. She pushed furniture around after it was delivered, hung towels in the bathrooms and prepared supper for him and his father three nights running. She and Jessie stood on stepladders and measured for window treatments, then put the airy curtains up when they arrived.

On his first night in the house, Micah gave an impromptu dinner party and Eli, Jessie, Landy and Nancy Burnside came. They laughed, told stories, ate pizza and drank beer. When everyone went home, Micah kissed Nancy and Jessie on the cheek, Landy brought up the rear, and he didn't kiss her at all, just gave her a long look. After that night, he hardly saw her at all.

She waved to him across the produce aisle at the grocery store, but by the time he carried his purchases through the checkout, her aged black Chevy was pulling out of the parking lot. He saw her on the River Walk most evenings at dusk, walking as fast as her hitching gait allowed. She and Eli were in and out of each other's houses, too. Sometimes one of Eli's numerous and sundry children accompanied her trek around the thumb, and the lapping river water would transmit the sound of her laughter to Micah as he sat on his back porch.

"I always liked that little girl," his father said one evening, and Micah looked up to see the setting sun embracing Landy, turning her hair the color of orange marmalade and making his heart ache in a place he hadn't known was there.

He thought then about asking her to go to dinner with him, maybe crossing the big bridge into Cincinnati to see a play, but later that night he saw Eli slip through the darkness to her house.

It was a good match—Eli and Landy. Micah told himself that, but then he sat silent and morose on the porch until he saw Eli go home.

The "Window Over the Sink" columns arrived in the mail every Friday, and he printed them in Saturday's Trib. People liked them. "Been there, done that, bought the damn T-shirt," they told him.

Plans for the newspaper were working out, coming together faster than he'd thought possible. Advertising and subscriptions were both on an upswing. The town clergymen took turns writing a short, inspirational piece every week. Mrs. Burnside did a rambling twenty inches or so on who was doing what. It was corny, she admitted, writing down when so-and-so's daughter from Ithaca, New York, visited with her two young sons and spoiled cocker spaniel, but people liked reading it and she had a good time compiling it. Micah liked her writing—and her—so well he offered her the receptionist's job and she took it, managing his news-paper office as efficiently as she had geometry class. Her coffee was good, too; his entire staff had threatened mutiny when, being the first one in the office one Monday morning, he made the coffee.

"This stuff," said Joe Carter mildly, "gives sludge a bad name." So Nancy made the coffee.

"Window Over the Sink" was the most popular of the columns, drawing the most reader comment. Everyone had his own idea of who Susan was, ranging from Jenny from the café to Micah's father—an idea that horrified Ethan. Micah had even looked at the back of one of the newspaper's checks that had been issued to Susan Billings, to see if her signature looked familiar. But the check was stamped with For Deposit Only and had been cashed without question at a local bank.

Micah considered for a while that the writer might be Landy. In the end, he didn't think so, because she had no children and her high-school heartthrob was dead. Susan wrote with a lightness of spirit that had left Landy one night on the stairs of her grandmother's house.

He didn't really know what Landy did, though. She worked at the realty sometimes, but not often. She sub-stitute-taught everything from kindergarten to senior English and occasionally waited tables during the lunch rush Down at Jenny's. She volunteered everywhere, clerking for the blood drive, reading aloud at Wee Care Preschool, and delivering Meals on Wheels.

He saw her in church, in the same pew as Jessie Titus Browning with Jessie's three children lined up between them. Sometimes, Landy wasn't at the service, and he wondered where she was until one Sunday he went to the basement restroom and found her presid-ing over the nursery.

When he caught sight of her that Sunday, Micah stood in the door of the big room that housed the nursery, not noticing the cribs, the changing table or the miniature table and chairs. Not even really seeing the six or seven preschoolers milling around the room.

He saw only Landy, standing with a baby on her hip. She swayed gently, crooning into the ear of the sobbing infant. Watching her, he remembered something his father had said once. "Equal rights or no, there's nothing in the world any prettier than a woman with a baby in her arms."

Pop had been right.

The woman looked up and saw him then, and smiled. "Good morning," she said. "Here."

Before he knew what was happening, she had plunked the weeping baby in his arms and was rummaging in a cupboard. "These kids are starving to death. They know they get treats down here, and Colby—he's the one you're holding—has kept me so busy I'm behind."

"Okay." Micah looked down at the wizened little face of the baby. "I'll try not to drop you if you'll quit crying, how does that sound?"

He stepped carefully between the toys that littered the carpeted floor and sat in a rocking chair, propping Colby up on his shoulder the way he'd seen countless women do. It couldn't be that hard, could it? The baby smelled good, and Micah breathed deep.

Landy handed out disgusting-looking fruit things to the children and began pouring juice out of a can into paper cups. "Sing to him," she suggested over her shoulder. "He likes it."

"You think so, huh," he grunted, but when Colby's whimpers became sobs again, he began to sing "Yellow Submarine" in a low voice.

Pretty soon, Colby stopped crying, and by the time Micah had finished "Hey, Jude" and was halfway through "A Hard Day's Night," the other children were quiet, too. They sat cross-legged on the floor and listened.

"That's classical music, my dad says," commented Lindsey, Eli's youngest. "My brother Max says it's just old."

The snort of laughter from the woman leaning against a changing table made Micah glad he'd come down the stairs, even though his hand was asleep and Colby's diaper had sprung a definite leak.

"Would you have dinner with me tonight?" he asked, not caring that all the children heard him and Lindsey was probably going to report to her father that his friend Micah was asking Landy for a date.

Landy started, and her cheeks turned pink, but she was smiling again when she answered. "Sure, if you'll sing 'Twist and Shout.' I always liked that."

"It's a date, Jess. What in the hell am I doing going on a date?" Clad in white cotton underwear, Landy paced between her closet and dressing table, so distracted that she didn't even think about her leg.

"Driving yourself crazy, I'd say," said Jessie, "and it's about time."

"He just looked so sweet, holding Colby and singing, I couldn't say no. But Blake used to be sweet, too, and if I'd said no more often, he'd probably still be alive."

"Landy—"

"It's true. Don't try and tell me it's not." Landy reached for the cup of tea that sat cooling on a table.

"Okay, I won't. But maybe if I'd told somebody the first time he ever hit you—after you smiled at Micah and told him good game—Blake would still be alive. Maybe if his parents hadn't blinded themselves to his violence, he'd still be alive. Maybe if the steps in your grandma's house hadn't been so steep, there wouldn't have been time for the gun to go off and he'd still be alive." Jessie's normally soft brown eyes snapped. "You going to live the rest of your life on maybes?"

Landy got up, going back to her closet. "Maybe," she said over her shoulder, and laughed when Jessie raised one finger in a universal gesture.

"Wear a dress." Jessie poured more tea.

"Oh, Jess, I don't think so." Landy looked down at the scars left by the surgeries on her leg. "This doesn't look too pretty."

Their eyes met in the mirror. "You're right. You've been hiding from who you are ever since Blake died," said Jessie. "Why stop now?"

Stung, Landy reached far into the closet and withdrew a hanger.

It looked like a basic "little black dress" until the wearer moved and hints of plum shimmered in its depths. Darts and seams made it fit as though it had been tailored for her, even though she'd bought it off the clearance rack at the boutique beside Down at Jenny's. She'd never worn it, but sometimes she would come into her room and try it on. She'd turn this way and that before the long mirror and imagine herself unscarred and free.

Maybe, just for tonight, that's what she could be.

She slid her feet into strappy black cloth heels and fastened silver hoops in her ears, a silver chain around her throat that nestled inside the scooped neckline of the dress, and a row of delicate bracelets that slipped up and down her arm and captured light when they moved.

"You look wonderful," said Jessie, her voice soft.

Landy looked into the mirror again, almost afraid there would be no reflection there because the Landy Wisdom who wore clothes like this no longer existed.

"It's really me," she said, swallowing sudden, ridiculous tears.

By the time she reached the bottom of the stairs, she knew the heels were a mistake. She already had one off when the doorbell rang, and she limped to answer, standing with her stockinged foot tucked behind her other leg.

"Hi," she said.

"Wow," he said.

She tugged her shoe back on. If she regretted it, so be it. "We should go," she said. "I'll turn back into a frump when the eleven o'clock news comes on."

"Never in a million years." He looked up at where Jessie stood on the stairs. "She have a curfew, Jess?"

She grinned at him. "Before daylight or else park in the garage. We don't want the neighbors talking."

"Eli would be parked on the porch waiting." Landy lifted a black cashmere stole from the newel post. "He runs the neighborhood watch," she explained to Micah.

"Is that all it is?"

"What else?" she asked, puzzled, but he was opening the door for her. "Later, Jess."

"I thought we'd go to the Overlook. It's warm enough to eat on the porch. That okay with you?" Micah seated her in the passenger side of his Blazer—giving her a boost when her skirt was too narrow for her to negotiate the step up—and pulled the seat belt up for her to fasten.

"It's my favorite place," she said, when he'd climbed in beside her. "I like your Blazer."

"My dad wanted me to bring his nice, conservative Buick. He said it was a much better choice for taking a lady out to dinner."

She adopted a haughty air. "That's all right. We debutantes are quite tolerant."

They were seated at a table beside the windows that looked out over the Ohio when Micah said, "I was crazy about you, you know."

Her eyes widened. "You didn't even like me."

"It made me mad that you couldn't see what a jerk Trent was, and I knew I'd never have enough money or prestige to ask you out, regardless of him."

"Oh, my goodness, no. You weren't even good enough to kiss my ring in those days." Anger and disappointment made her voice wobble, which made her even angrier. "Take a look at me, all right?" She gestured toward her body with open palms. "I have wrinkles and scars and a gimpy leg. Most of my grandmother's money paid for a lawsuit after I killed my husband. Here's your debutante, Micah."

Fury gave flash to her quiet prettiness, and Micah enjoyed her anger even as he did a little internal squirming because he was almost certain it was justified.

"You're right," he said. He picked up the wine bottle that sat between them and poured more into both their glasses. "I'm sorry. Coming back to Taft seems to have brought out the angry young pain in the ass in me."

She laughed, as he'd hoped she would. "I'm sorry for blowing up, too," she said. "Shall we start over?" She extended her hand. "I'm Landy Wisdom."

He took her hand and raised it to his lips. "Micah Walker," he said. "Very happy to make your acquaintance. Lovely weather we're having, isn't it?"

She beamed at him, her eyes tilting, and he felt his heart do a flip-flop.

Over the main course, he asked, "Do you think Nancy Burnside has designs on my father?"

Landy dropped her fork. "Designs? Mrs. Burnside? I'm not sure, but I think that borders on blasphemy. She's a geometry teacher. Isn't that like a nun?"

"She *was* a geometry teacher," he corrected. "She drank beer at my housewarming party. That's not nun-like."

"She was just being polite," she scoffed. "Good grief, she's been widowed forever."

He took a sip of wine, looking at her over the glass. "I think it would be great, starting over in your sixties."

"It doesn't bother you, thinking of your father being with someone besides your mother?"

"No. At least not as much as the idea of him being alone the rest of his life bothers me."

"Jessie and Eli and you and I are all alone," she said. "Not everyone's meant to walk two by two."

"No, but my father is. There are holes in his life that definitely can't be filled by a thirty-eight-year-old single son who makes bad coffee."

There were holes in her life, too. Great empty gaps where self-confidence and two good legs used to be. Not to mention waking in the middle of the night with longing singing through her veins and making her heart pound painfully hard. Though she hadn't always enjoyed sex with Blake, she missed the kissing, cuddling and full body contact that came before it, the illusion of closeness that came after.

She looked across the table at Micah and acknowledged the attraction she'd felt since first seeing him again in the church basement. She was honest enough to admit that the attraction went back as far as Taft High School, when she'd smiled at Micah even knowing Blake would be angry.

She would like, she knew, to kiss and cuddle with Micah, to sleep in his arms and wake beside him. She'd like to cook his breakfast wearing nothing but his shirt, the way they always did in movies. It would do an admirable job of filling some of the holes of being alone.

But, between the cuddling and breakfast came the

act itself, the physical invasion that meant she was being overpowered. Micah would expect that, but she would never be overpowered again.

After dinner, they sauntered through the gardens of the Overlook. Landy's leg was killing her, and her limp became more pronounced despite her best efforts.

"You're hurting, aren't you?" he said suddenly, and seated her on a path-side bench before she knew what was happening. He knelt before her, lifting her foot to his thigh and slipping off her shoe. "Why didn't you say something? Here." He handed the shoe to her and straightened, lifting her into his arms and moving toward the parking lot.

"I'm fine," she insisted, holding herself away from him, hoping to stave off the warmth that emanated from his body along with the fresh scent of soap. "It just does that sometimes."

"Ms. Wisdom." He stopped walking and scowled down into her face. Reflections from the muted lights that lined the path danced in his eyes. "I am trying my best to use the manners my mama taught me. The least you can do is go along with it and maybe, just maybe, I won't drop you."

"Oh." She relaxed in spite of herself, allowing the warmth to flow over and through her. "Your mama would be proud," she said, as they approached the Blazer.

"I hope so." He opened the car door, propped his foot on the inside running board so that her backside rested on his thigh, lowered his head and kissed her.

Oh, yes, was all she had time to think before her senses took over. This wasn't passion as she knew it. There was no demand in the heat of his lips. His eyes had been clear and bright before they closed, not fogged by alcohol or some other mind-altering drug. Although his arms tightened as the kiss deepened, no hand pushed against her breast or thrust beneath the skirt of her dress. When his tongue sought entry into her mouth, she denied it, but he didn't end the kiss in fury or disgust. He raised his head, smiled at her and lowered it again.

This time, when his tongue slid across the seam of her lips, she opened them. The age-old dance was slow and warm and tasted sweetly of wine and coffee and something else. She felt a sensation between her thighs that she hadn't felt in—oh, so very long. Her breasts were sensitized, the soft cloth that covered them feeling scratchy even though it wasn't.

"That wasn't part of what my mama taught me," he said when the kiss ended.

Chapter Four

Window Over the Sink, Taft Tribune: *Trust is something you lose when you grow up, eroded by the hurts and betrayals that are part of everyone's life from the time you find out your folks lied about Santa Claus. But every spring, when the green has made us forget the browns of winter and kites make colorful stars in the daytime sky, we learn once again to trust. We know Taft will clamor with the sounds of lawnmowers on Saturday afternoons, another class will be preparing to graduate from Taft High and everyone will be sweeping their porches just to have an excuse to be outside.*

I said once that there is a price to be paid for

spring, and there is, but that regaining of trust—
even if it's temporary—is worth the cost.

"Neighborhood watch, huh?" Micah lifted a hand to return Eli's wave as his neighbor jogged toward Landy's house. "Seems to me he only watches one house."

The thought that he was sitting on his porch spying on people and talking to himself entered his mind, and he returned his attention to the golf clubs he was re-gripping.

He was wrapping tape around the shaft of the seven iron when a voice said, "You could at least offer me a beer," and he raised his eyes to see Eli standing on the brick path that led to the River Walk.

"I could," Micah agreed, and looked down at the roll of tape in his hand. "Or you could go in and get the beer and we could both have one."

"Once a sixth man, always a sixth man," Eli complained, walking past him and into the house.

Micah grinned at nothing, thinking Eli hadn't stayed long at Landy's house. Not that it was any of his business. It wasn't. Really.

"Lindsey tells me you and Landy had a date."

"Why am I not surprised?" Micah took the bottle Eli offered. "Did she also tell you I sang Beatles songs in church and little Colby Whatshisname peed all over me?"

"Oh, yes." Eli sat down. "Lindsey's very thorough. Her older siblings have threatened to clamp her lips together with Super Glue."

"Did you stop by to tell me you don't want me to see Landy anymore?" Micah asked bluntly.

Eli's eyebrows shot up so high they disappeared under the dark blond hair that fell over his forehead. "Huh?" He set his beer on the porch floor with a little bang. "Why in the pocket of Joseph's coat would I do that?"

Micah glared at him. "Well, because—why in the what?"

Eli looked abashed and ridiculously young. "For a minister," he said, "I have an alarming tendency toward swearing. In order to keep their father employed and out of their hair, my two oldest children gave me a list of curse alternatives. Some of them stuck." He picked up his beer. "But don't change the subject. Why did you think I would mind you seeing Landy?"

"Well." It was Micah's turn to be embarrassed, and he was. "You go over there a lot, all times of the day and night. You walk in without knocking. You're both single adults. I just thought...." He let his voice trail off.

Eli shook his head sadly. "A big-city reporter, award-winning, no less, and you jump to conclusions like you were still a running back on a high school football team. Lord, Lord," he said prayerfully, looking up, "what is to become of this lamb of Yours? This black sheep, I mean. I understand that the Beatles songs in Your house were okay—You have John Lennon and George Harrison with You, after all—but couldn't You just give him a little guidance down the path of common sense?" He waited, head cocked as though listening, then gave Micah a doleful look. "He says He did, but you went the wrong way. Again."

"Elijah St. John, you are an unmitigated asshole." But Micah was laughing.

"I try," said Eli modestly.

"If you aren't seeing Landy, why *do* you go over there all the time?" Micah demanded. So much for minding his own business, but there were limits, after all.

The smile stayed on Eli's face, but dimmed in the green eyes. "We're friends," he said. "She's gone through a rotten few years. A rotten many years, really."

"I know." When Eli didn't continue, Micah was silent. He had been a reporter long enough to understand about confidentiality even when it was unspoken. He had, in the past, pushed people to the very limits of their discretion. Somewhere along the line, he'd lost his taste for that—at least in his personal life.

It was time to change the subject. But not necessarily to mind his own business.

"What about you?" he asked quietly. "Did you have some bad years, too? You're a divorced minister with six kids. I doubt that was an easy thing to become."

Sadness slid over Eli's features like a mask. The expression was so out of place on the usually smiling face that Micah felt as if the sun had suddenly disappeared behind a cloud. He got to his feet. "Be right back," he said, and went into the house.

When he came back out, carrying a bag of potato chips, Eli's face was clear again, though there was a pensive look in his eyes.

"Remember," he said, "how you used to call Landy the town debutante?"

Micah nodded, flinching. "I've also made that mistake in the past couple of weeks."

"Well, I went to Princeton, remember, and I met a real one." Eli shook his head. "White dress, curtseying, the whole bit. Dee was my roommate's sister and I met her when I went home with him on some weekends. It was like being in a different world, you know, where people actually *do* dress for dinner, and she was the very best part of it.

"She really liked the idea of cultivating the country boy and we got married the week after I graduated. It wasn't until we were on our honeymoon that she found out she couldn't talk me out of being a minister. Still, it was okay as long as we lived in the Hamptons and had a big, social church. She was a good minister's wife, generous with her time and money both. We had the first two kids—Max and Josh—and entered them in nursery school before they were even born. It was okay," he repeated, looking down at the beer in his hand.

"What made it not okay anymore?"

"She got pregnant again, wanted an abortion, I said no. She agreed to have the child, finally—that's Wendy—and loved her after she was born, but it changed something between us. I didn't feel the same about Dee and she stayed angry. Then her brother—my old roommate—and his wife were killed in an accident. Dee was distraught, of course—her whole family was— but no one wanted their kids. We'd agreed to be their guardians without ever once thinking what that entailed.

Dee wanted to allow some rich, childless couple to adopt them, but I couldn't do that. Hence, I got Ben, Little Eli and Lindsey, but lost my marriage in the process."

He looked up, smiling again. "I moved them all here to rebuild, and it's worked out well."

Micah sipped his beer silently, then set it down and concentrated on wrapping tape around the shaft of his six iron. He was angry with Eli's ex-wife, and he wanted to tell his friend she was no great loss; he could do better.

"What's Jessie's story?" he asked instead.

Eli's shrug was elaborately casual. "She's a nurse who was married to a doctor who died of a heart attack."

Something in his eyes alerted Micah that once again, Eli was fudging. "She's a nice woman."

Eli got up, brushing potato chip crumbs from his shirt. "She's okay. I need to go. I'm umpiring at Wendy's softball game. Now there's a job that ought to get me a father-of-the-year award."

"More likely to get you lynched," said Micah, laughing and completely failing to notice his friend's sudden speculative expression.

Which is how he found himself in a half-squat behind home plate yelling "Stee-rike one!" while demure young ladies in baseball caps and ponytails kicked dust at him.

She'd been so involved with the shape of his mouth and how well it fit over hers that Landy hadn't taken the shape of Micah's backside into account. When he assumed the position of home plate umpire at the game in which Jessie's and Eli's daughters were playing, she had a chance to correct the omission.

The view was admirable.

"Breathe. You're turning blue," Jessie mumbled. She sighed. "He does look fine, doesn't he?"

"Yes, he does." Landy looked sideways at her friend, seeing the wistful expression on her face. "You know, Jess," she said carefully, "I don't have any claims on him. We just went out once, is all."

Jessie gave her a blank look. "What in the name of Noah's ark are you talking about?"

"Nothing." Landy grinned at her, unable to quash the ripple of gladness Jessie's reply created. "You've been around Eli too long. You're starting to talk like him. Is there anything you'd like me to know?"

"Oh, please." The look this time was wilting. "I loved, married and lost one workaholic. I don't think I care to go through it again. Eli and I are just friends, thank you very much, and we will remain that. Except for when we're being enemies, that is."

The subject of their conversation came up the bleachers and sat between them, casting a longing gaze at Landy's popcorn that made her lift her shoulders in resignation and hand him the bag. "Garbage gut."

"You need to talk to Micah," he said, taking Jessie's soft drink and lifting it to his lips. "He's suspicious of me coming to your house, and I can't lie to him."

"He's a reporter," said Landy. "We can't tell him. How can you suggest such a thing?"

"He's my friend," he reminded her, his gaze level on hers. "I trust him, and it's time you trusted somebody."

"I've been there and done that," she said, her voice feeling jagged in her throat. "I do trust him, to a certain extent, but not about Safe Harbor Railroad. It's too important to too many people."

"I'm not forgetting," he said, "but maybe it's time you did. Some things, at least." Eli stopped, his eyes narrowing as he watched the field. "He just called Wendy out. Doesn't friendship mean anything in this world?"

Jessie looked toward the sky, a cloudless blue expanse. "It'll be a terrible waste of good weather if no one cooks out tonight."

"I will," said Landy immediately. "I'm probably the only one whose grill is clean anyway." She prepared to leave. "Will you invite Micah for me? And his father and Nancy, too, if they'd like to come."

She was standing beside the grill in her backyard when Micah came down the River Walk. She wore a towel on her head and a robe and had a cordless phone tucked between her shoulder and her ear as she poked at the grill.

When he came close, she looked up and flashed him a smile, but something like guilt crossed her eyes. Something furtive that made him feel like a snoop and an interloper. He frowned, not liking the sensation, and walked past her to put the beer and soft drinks he carried into the cooler that sat on the end of the picnic table.

A moment later, she said, "Hey, Micah," and he turned. She was putting the phone in the pocket of her robe. "How are you at starting fires?" she asked.

They were at least five feet apart, but the tension arced between them so obviously that he almost expected to see sparks. This hadn't been the kind of fire she meant, but it was there nonetheless.

"Well," he said, "I never was a Boy Scout."

She looked so wonderful standing there. No makeup covered the dark shadows under her eyes or filled in the little brackets that pain had dug around her mouth, but her smile lit her face. It made her look younger, as did the anxiety behind it.

He wanted to kiss her again, and the drooping shawl collar of her robe showed the shadowed beginnings of her breasts, making him want to do more than kiss her. He even took a step in her direction, then stopped, suddenly realizing that her tension wasn't the same as his.

Anxiety. He'd already thought the word, but its meaning hadn't come through then. It did now. Her tension was sexual, as his was, but it didn't feel good, as his did. His was anticipatory; hers was filled with dread.

Oh, God. Oh, dear sweet God. She was afraid of him.

He cleared his throat. "Your hair looks fetching that way, and I like your outfit," he said, his voice sounding gravelly, "but if you want to finish getting ready, I'll see what I can do with the fire."

"Thank you," she said, and turned and fled.

* * *

"I acted like a freaking idiot," she told Jessie, tossing salad with a violence that had iceberg lettuce littering the counter, the floor and Jessie's arm when she stood too close.

Jessie didn't crack a smile. "That's no act. Stand up straight."

"I can't."

Worry crossed her friend's features, and Landy was sorry she'd answered so abruptly. "It just hurts some today, is all," she assured her.

"Right." Jessie reached into the cupboard over her head and found the kitchen bottle of pain relievers. "Are you taking these a lot?" she asked, running a glass of water and handing it to Landy.

"More than I'd like," Landy admitted, "but not a dangerous amount." She swallowed the pills. "What am I going to do, Jess? He's so attractive, and I get goose bumps just being in the same room with him, but if he touches me—I mean *really* touches me, I'm going to freeze up. I know it." She tossed salad with frustrated abandon. "Why does the actual act mean so much to men?"

"Not just to men." Jessie washed vegetables, her expression pensive. "The 'act,' as you call it, is wonderful. I'm so sorry you never had the opportunity to know how wonderful. And," she added, shaking a carrot at Landy so that droplets of water sprayed them both, "you never will if you don't work on this fear."

"Work on it," Landy repeated. "As in what? Writing

a report? Driving everyone nuts by talking ad nauseum about my hang-ups? Asking Micah to be an experiment?"

Jessie glared at her. "Maybe," she said. Still scowling, she demanded, "Where's the damn vegetable tray?"

"I have it," said a meek voice from behind them, and they both swung on Eli.

"How long have you been listening?" Landy asked.

He adopted an injured air. "Not long enough, evidently. I didn't hear one thing that was interesting. Holy sh—shmoly, Landy, what have you been doing with that salad? It's all the way from one end of the kitchen to the other."

"Take it," she ordered, plunking the salad bowl into Eli's still-open hands and giving the sectioned vegetable platter to Jessie. "We'll be right out."

He moved toward the door, but stopped before he got there. "You might try it," he said quietly, "the experiment thing, I mean. Not all men are pigs. Not all reporters are untrustworthy."

Micah was standing at the edge of her brick sidewalk with Lindsey in his arms when Landy went outside. "Your walk's coming apart," he said.

"I know. It's on this spring's to-do list." She stroked Lindsey's strawberry blond hair back from her face. "Hungry, Linds?"

"Oh, you've met my new girlfriend?" Micah looked at her past the child's face, his eyes warm. "Be careful. She's the jealous type."

"He's silly, Aunt Landy," Lindsey announced, planting

a noisy, wet kiss on his cheek and pushing herself out of his arms. "Let me go, Uncle Mike. The hot dogs are done."

Landy watched the little girl run to join her siblings and Jessie's children around a platter mounded with hot dogs. "Uncle Mike, huh? You've made a conquest."

"Oh," he said, "I'm a whiz with the five-year-old set. And Wendy and Jessie's girl Hannah assured me I didn't do too bad as an umpire." His hand lifted, pushing her hair back from her face in much the same way as she had Lindsey's, although his touch was much more tentative. "How am I doing with the thirty-so-methings?"

His hand lingered at her hairline, then slipped down to cup her cheek. She looked up at him, and it seemed that she could become lost in the foggy depths of his gray eyes. And she wanted to. She wanted to be lost in that way that happened to other women but eluded her.

When she spoke, her voice was thready. "Not bad," she said. "Not bad at all."

Chapter Five

Window Over the Sink, Taft Tribune: *Sometimes life goes so smoothly, you're lulled into a false sense of security. You know, the mortgage is paid ahead, you've lost the ten pounds you'd gained since the last high school reunion. The sunset reflects its palette of colors on the Twilight and gives you heart's ease at the end of the day and all is blissfully right with the world.*

Then, in one short day—or perhaps only a moment—it all goes to hell in a hand basket.

He waited till everyone else had gone to take his leave. Then he took her into his arms and kissed Landy until his legs felt like scrambled eggs.

For a moment, she trembled, and he expected her to draw away, but she didn't. She just looked up at him in the flickering light from citronella torches and said, "Lindsey wouldn't like this."

Do you? Your heart's beating as fast as mine, but I don't know if it's from excitement or fear. He tried to ask her the question silently, but there were no answers in her face. Only more questions.

"Didn't you notice?" His voice sounded funny to his own ears. He was reminded of coming back to earth after a heavy make-out session at the drive-in that used to be on the edge of town. His heart was pumping like crazy and he felt flushed and warm, even though the evening had cooled.

It had been a while since he'd felt seventeen.

"She attached herself to my father," he said, his voice still uneven. "I think she has an older man fetish."

She chuckled, and the husky laughter weakened his legs still further. Keeping her in his arms, he lowered himself to the porch swing. "Of course," he said, "I'm an older man, too." He lifted her hand, setting it palm-to-palm against his, and captured her gaze. "Hopefully wiser."

When he lowered his hand, it drifted, almost as though by accident, against the swell of her breast, and lingered there. He kept the touch light; he could scarcely feel her softness against his skin. Then he kissed her again, a leisurely blending of taste and touch and elusive scent.

"Oh, yes," she whispered when the kiss ended and he had withdrawn his hand from her breast, "definitely wiser."

She wanted more. He saw it in her eyes as clearly as he saw the shadows underneath them. But the ache in his groin persuaded him it was time to abstain—he needed to stop before she became frightened and he went crazy.

"I have to go," he said, and his voice was again the one from the drive-in. "You'll be okay?"

He heard the telephone ring inside the house, and she lifted her head sharply. "I need to get that." She pushed herself to her feet, then leaned back down to kiss him. "Go home, Micah. Thank you."

He was halfway to his house before he realized she hadn't answered him when he'd asked if she'd be okay.

And what had she been thanking him for?

"The mother's in the hospital, just for tonight. She doesn't want Social Services to take her kids." Jessie's voice was terse and tired.

"Do you need me to come and get them?"

"Eli's here. He'll bring them." Jessie hesitated, and Landy sensed her concern.

"What is it?" she asked, heading toward the stairway. "Do I need the crib out?"

"No, they're four and five. Both girls. It's just getting a little scary, Landy. I'm afraid it's only a matter of time till someone picks up on the fact that Eli and I keep showing up at your house in the middle of the night with strangers in tow. What good will the Railroad be if none of us are safe?"

Landy stopped on the landing to lean against the

wall and catch her breath. Her leg hurt badly tonight. She thought of Micah, who had seen Eli coming to her house late at night. The thought, combined with Jessie's words, sent a shiver of dread up her spine.

"Well," she said briskly, "we'll cross that bridge when we come to it. Or fall in, whichever comes first."

"There's one good thing about that."

"What's that?"

"From what I hear, debutantes float. They don't sink like rocks the way us common folk do."

"Jessie, have I ever told you you're a bitch?"

"Many times." Her friend's deep chuckle was comforting. "Many, many times."

Landy disconnected the phone with the sound of Jessie's laughter still in her ear and continued up the stairs, going into the pretty guest room at the end of the hall. Only it wouldn't really be just a guest room tonight, but a depot on the Safe Harbor Railroad, an underground group assembled for the protection of battered women and children.

She took the hand-pieced quilts off the twin beds and replaced them with Winnie the Pooh comforters, hung matching towels in the bathroom and got the little white step out of the closet to place before the vanity. She plugged in night lights and searched through dresser drawers for pajamas likely to please little girls. In the hall, she stopped the pendulum of the grandfather clock. Its noise soothed her at night, but had been known to frighten young passengers on the Railroad.

Downstairs again, she made peanut butter and jelly

sandwiches, poured milk into plastic glasses with the Little Mermaid cavorting around the outside, and placed Oreos on a plate.

Then she sat down to wait.

Eli was going to Landy's in the middle of the night again.

Micah watched, frowning, as his friend came up the River Walk. His walk was slow tonight, neither the stride that told anyone who knew him that he was lost in thought nor his usual purposeful jog with head and shoulders back.

He was carrying something, and it looked as though Lindsey walked at his side.

Micah frowned. Lindsey had a bedtime; he had been at Eli's when she tried to charm her way out of it. He had, in fact, been coerced into reading three chapters of *Understood Betsy* instead of one because "Uncle Mike" wasn't nearly as immune to her wheedling as her father was.

Unease made the hair on the back of his neck stand up the way it did when Lucas Trent stared at him. Maybe something was wrong. Maybe Eli needed help. Micah got to his feet and started toward the edge of the verandah, then stopped. If Eli needed him, he would ask.

There was work to be done anyway. Micah hadn't even started the editor's column for this Saturday's paper, and what was worse was that he didn't have a clue as to what he was going to write about. For a minute, he envied Susan Billings, whoever she was. All she had to do was whip out seven hundred words and mail or fax them into the office. She didn't have to show up for work and her columns didn't have to be meaningful or even well-written. They just had to be fun to read.

Which they were, he admitted. Nancy photocopied "Window Over the Sink" when it came in and shoved a copy into every newspaper employee's mail slot. It was the only thing that garnered as much attention in the office as high school baseball and who'd lost his ass on the gambling boat up river.

He opened his laptop on the kitchen table and poured a glass of iced tea. Propping his glasses on his nose, he began to type, looking toward the window often. From where he sat, he had a good view of the River Walk.

Ethan came in while he was working, singing "Heartbreak Hotel" and playing an imaginary guitar. His thick gray hair was mussed, and there was a light in his pewter-colored eyes that Micah hadn't seen for a long time. He tried not to mind that it was back.

"I don't even want to know what you've been doing," he said.

His father turned from the refrigerator. "That's good, because it's none of your business." He poured tea for himself, then came over to refill Micah's glass. "I loved your mother so much," he said in a husky voice, "and being able to talk about her to someone who understands—it's so great, son, because I'm talking about her life and not about her death."

Micah thought of his mother, thought about how much she'd loved his father. She'd be happy to see him like this, bellowing out old Elvis Presley songs and swinging his still-trim hips.

"I'm glad, Pop," Micah said quietly, and he was. He was. He had no business being otherwise.

He deleted the three hundred words he'd already written and started over. He had no idea how a seasoned writer could compose such crap.

"Is that Eli?"

Ethan's question brought Micah's head up so quickly his glasses fell to the table. He peered through the window. "Yeah," he said. "He must have gone back down to Landy's for something."

And he came back alone. No burden in his arms; no little one at his side. Of course, Lindsey could have spent the night with Landy—they were crazy about each other. That was probably it.

The unease he'd felt earlier returned, and he ran smoothing fingers through the hair that was standing on end from earlier hand-routs. He got up, feeling the need to move, and considered following Eli, but his friend was jogging on his trip toward home.

"What's wrong?" asked Ethan. "You're wearing your on-a-story face. I haven't seen that since you left Lexington."

"I'm just edgy."

A couple of hundred truly awful words later, the phone rang, sounding loud in the quiet room, and Micah snatched it up. "Walker."

"Micah?" It was Landy's voice. She sounded shaky. "I'm sorry to bother you, but I seem to be having a little trouble climbing the stairs and you're the closest. Could you come and help me?"

"Stay put. I'll be right there." He started to hang up the phone, but something—maybe it was his on-a-story intuition, for all he knew—made him ask, "Do you want me to drive or walk? How uncomfortable are you?"

"Walk, please." The answer was instant, with something like panic thinning her husky voice. "Just let yourself in the back door."

He put down the phone. "She needs help."

Ethan handed him his jacket. "Cell phone's in the pocket," he said. "Call if you need me to do anything."

"Thanks, Pop."

Micah sprinted toward Landy's bungalow. The windbreaker he wore carried his father's scent, a mixture of wintergreen Life Savers and cherry pipe tobacco, and the aroma was as reassuring as it had always been.

Women trusted Ethan. From Micah's mother all the way to Lindsey St. John, they knew he would never betray them. Micah felt a pang of sharp envy, knowing the same words couldn't be applied to him. Women liked him all right, and little Lindsey flirted with him with blue eyes that seemed the size of dinner plates in her pretty child's face, but it was other men, like Ethan and Eli, that they trusted.

Except....

When she needed help, Landy Wisdom had called on him.

Landy had seen the term "simmering rage" in books and had always liked it. She'd wanted to use it in a sentence the way she used to do with the vocabulary words assigned in school, and had created an opportunity once, one that had earned her slashing red lines on a composition. If she was being truthful, rage didn't usually simmer in her experience; it exploded.

But her leg felt like simmering rage. Spiraling fire climbed from her ankle to her hip. She knew just as sure as the Twilight flowed into the Ohio that when she moved it, the rage of pain was going to explode and the little swirls of pain were going to become an inferno.

"Please," she whispered, "don't let me yell and wake those children up there. And please," she added for good measure, "don't let me make a complete fool of myself in front of Micah."

She felt so sleepy, and she held her eyes open wide as she tried to remember how many pain relievers she'd taken today. Not enough to knock her out or make it seem as if she'd attempted suicide, she was sure, but how many?

Maybe if she just closed her eyes, the pain would ebb, and when Micah arrived, she could just pull herself to her feet and say, False alarm, but thanks for coming. With a bright smile, of course.

"Landy?"

She heard his voice, but couldn't make her eyes open again. She tried to speak, but though her mouth moved, no sound came out. *I'll bet I look like a fish.*

"Landy?" he said again. "You don't have to talk if it's hard, but try to open your eyes."

Feeling as though the lids were being pried apart, she forced her eyes to open and willed her lips into what she hoped passed for a smile.

"Hi, Uncle Mike," she whispered.

He lifted her carefully, and in spite of the pain in her leg, she was conscious that she wore nothing under her robe and nightgown. In response to the thought, she felt her nipples grow erect and it was all she could do not to squirm in his arms as he carried her to her room.

"It's happened before," she insisted, when she was sitting in her bed, her back against the pillows and her legs stretched out in front of her, "and there's nothing they can do except operate on my leg again. I'll go that route when I have to, not before."

"When will that be?" he argued, resting a hip on the edge of the bed. "Maybe after you've sat on your landing for three days because you can't move? What if you hadn't had your phone in your pocket?"

"It goes away," she said calmly. "Usually within just a few minutes. It lasted a little longer tonight, is all."

He looked at her, and she knew he was seeing the shadows under her eyes and the lines around her mouth that seemed to deepen whenever she had pain. "I think I should stay with you," he said flatly.

She fluttered her eyelashes at him. "Why, Mr. Walker, how you do take on."

He grinned at her. "Don't bother with the Melanie Wilkes act. I think you're Scarlett, through and through."

"Actually," she said with a sigh, "I'm more like Careen, Scarlett's sister who was scared of her own shadow." *And became a nun.* She smiled, although she doubted it was convincing. "Go on home, Micah. I'll be fine. Promise. And thank you for rescuing me."

"In a little bit." He waited until she was nearly asleep before he rose, obviously reluctant to leave her. "You've got everything you need?"

"Everything."

He kissed her, rubbing his mouth gently on hers. "I knew it," he murmured. "You're Scarlett, all right."

Chapter Six

Window Over the Sink, Taft Tribune: *This morning, my neighbor three houses down shook her finger in my son's face and hollered at him, then marched him home. This, I thought, is one of the worst parts of living in a small town. Everybody knows your business, everybody could raise your kids better than you, everybody...well, you know what I mean.*

A little while ago, the same neighbor came over and brought me a bouquet of lilacs and apologized for yelling at my little darling, but he'd run into the street without looking and scared her to death.

That's when I remembered one of the best

*parts of living in a small town. Everybody knows
your business, everybody cares about your kids,
everybody...well, you know what I mean.*

Micah was late to work in the morning. He'd been unable to sleep after returning home the night before, had brewed an entire pot of hot water this morning before he realized he'd forgotten to add coffee to the filter basket, and later had been caught by both the town's red lights. Plus, at some point in his sleeplessness, he'd gotten up and finished the editor's column. More crap. It was not a good way to start the day.

To make matters worse, Allison Scott wasn't at work. "My mother's ill again," she said on the phone. "I'm in Lexington. I'll be back in a couple of days."

There was something in her voice he couldn't identify, and Micah frowned. He wanted to say, *Are you all right? Can I help?* But he didn't. "We'll get by. Not much going on here, anyway. Give our best to your mother. Do you have anything that we need to cover?"

"The civic theatre play's tonight. *Steel Magnolias.* The tickets are under the corner of my blotter. Maybe one of the stringers would like to see it and do a review."

"I'll go," said Micah, though he certainly hadn't meant to. "Eli has a kid or two in it, anyway, and Nancy's doing Shirley MacLaine's part. She borrowed Pop's bib overalls for the role and I want to see her in them."

Allison's laughter sounded tired. "Thanks, Boss. I'll see you Monday at the latest."

"Stay as long as she needs you, kiddo. Like I said, we'll get by."

As soon as he'd hung up, he lifted the receiver again.

"How are you this morning?" he asked when Landy answered.

"I'm fine, but thanks again for rescuing me."

"How do you feel about civic theatre?" he asked.

"I played Annie in *Annie Get Your Gun* in high school and you can ask that? How *can* you?"

"I don't remember that."

"Neither does anyone else, and that's a very good thing. However, I still have a soft spot for local theatre. Why?"

"I've got a couple of tickets for tonight's performance. Would you like to go with me? We could fold our arms across our chests and scowl at Nancy being Miz Ouiser. I'll even," he added generously, "throw in a ticket for the cake raffle."

"Oh, well, by all means. I couldn't even consider a date who wouldn't respect my sweet tooth."

"Is that a yes? Because if it's not, I'm going to ask Lindsey to go with me and she has to be home by eight-thirty. We couldn't even stay for the cake raffle."

"It's a yes," she said. "What time should I be ready?"

He arranged to pick her up and cradled the telephone. When he looked up, everyone in the newspaper office was staring at him. "What?"

Nobody answered, just looked away quickly, except for Nancy Burnside. She eyed him, her gaze pure speculation.

"Don't you have some obituaries to type, Miz Ouiser?" he asked pleasantly.

"Nobody died."

"Recipes?"

"Done."

"Ads?"

"Done."

"If you can't stay busy, maybe we don't need a receptionist. Maybe you should go back over to the high school and substitute teach. Terrorize all those little juvenile delinquents instead of me."

"The coffee's done, too."

He glowered at her. "Couldn't you at least *act* concerned?"

She grinned cheekily at him. "You've threatened my job at least once a day ever since I got here, except for the days you actually fired me. I'm starting to enjoy it."

He laughed, getting up and walking with her to the break area where the coffee was indeed ready. "So why the staring in there?" he asked, jerking his thumb over his shoulder toward the news room. "I was starting to think my fly was unzipped."

She poured coffee into the mug that had "Boss" inscribed on it in big red letters and handed it to him. "Well, you're a good boss, but you still have that city demeanor about you. You use bigger words than we do, wear more expensive clothes and you separate yourself from our personal lives. When we heard you laughing on that call just now, we saw a side to you I haven't seen in twenty years and the others had *never* seen. It was kind of nice."

"What do you mean, separate myself? I don't do that."

"Okay." She gestured toward the desk that was the advertising department. "What's his name?"

"Joe."

"Married?"

"I think so."

"Kids?"

His mind drew a blank. Did Joe Carter have kids? Hadn't he seen him somewhere with whole flock of them? Or had that been at the Little League park, where there were kids everywhere who didn't seem to belong to anybody?

"I don't know," he admitted.

"You should."

He thought for a moment about what she'd said, sipping coffee he was sure Jenny from the café would cheerfully kill to be able to brew.

"His life is his business," he said. "Unless he does something newsworthy, or has something newsworthy done to him, I'm not going to be a part of his personal life."

"You already are."

"Damn it, Nancy—"

"Watch your language, Mr. Walker." She rapped him sharply on the arm. "You are a part of his life because you're his employer. His livelihood is in your hands. In order to have a comfortable working relationship, you need to have his trust and he needs to feel that he has yours."

"He does," Micah answered instantly. "He does a great job."

"He undoubtedly knows that, but you need to tell him. And do you know that he wants to write, too? He takes classes at the community college, has for a long time. That's something you need to encourage."

"I gave him a raise. He's making twenty percent more than he was when I came here."

"I gave you A's in geometry. I also told you I thought you did a good job and were a kick-ass running back, although I didn't use those exact words. Which thing do you remember and which thing inspired your trust?"

"I remember you telling me how good I did," he admitted, then added, "but I still don't trust you."

"They remind me of you," said Micah as they exited the high-school auditorium where the civic players performed.

"Who does?" Since they were walking amid a crowd of teenagers in baggy jeans with their bodies pierced in myriad places, she looked up in confusion.

He held open the door that led outside, guiding her through with a hand on her back. "The women in *Steel Magnolias*. I know you're not southern, but you've got that same strong core. You're scared of things, but you don't let fear take over your life." His fingers splayed wide and she felt their heat from her bra to her waist. "Outside, you're soft."

"Mushy," she corrected. "It comes with age and lack of exercise. And I'm scared of everything." When he dropped his hand, the early May air was suddenly too cool, and she suppressed a shiver.

"Not soft like that. Maybe gentle would be a better word. Do you think I separate myself from people?"

Where had that come from? Well, at least they weren't talking about her anymore; that was a good thing. "Sure, you do," she said. "You're a reporter—it's natural for you to be better at listening than talking."

"I talk all the time, especially when people are watching TV. Drives them nuts." He opened the door of the Blazer and helped her inside. "Watch your leg."

"You talk," she said, when he was under the wheel, "but you don't say anything. About yourself, I mean. We all know you were in Lexington for a long time, but nothing else. Where have you been, who do you know, who have you loved?" She grinned at him. "Who *are* you?"

"I've been everywhere I wanted to go, met a lot of people and knew a few, and loved—" He stopped, and his smile faded into thoughtfulness. "I've loved," he said carefully, "but in the past."

"What happened?"

"Her name was Jill. I met her my junior year and we got engaged that summer." He started the car and sat staring through the windshield at the people still coming into the parking lot. "She was always in a hurry for everything, wanted to get married right away, have kids right away, buy a nice little house in the suburbs."

"Sounds good to me. You didn't want that?"

"Not then. I wanted it later, when I'd been the places and met the people you asked about. So, now she lives in Cairo, Illinois, with her husband and two kids. We exchange Christmas cards and call each other on our birthdays and Ben and I play golf and drink beer together when we go back to Homecoming Weekend. They didn't ask me to be a godfather to either of the boys because they didn't think I'd welcome the responsibility, but I'm in charge of buying baseball mitts."

"Do you have regrets?"

"Sometimes." He set the car in motion, pulling into the street in front of the school. "I look at Eli's menagerie and am sorry I don't have a few kids of my own to buy baseball gloves for, and I remember how my mom and dad were together and wish I could have that. But I know myself well enough to understand that I'm not good husband and father material. I like my own way too well. I like a quiet and neat house. I don't want to watch TV through sticky hand prints on the screen. I want to be able to go away and leave the computer on without worrying about someone hitting the delete key."

Landy thought of Britt and Andie, the little girls she'd left at her house with Jessie. They were blue-eyed and blond, so sweet that when she'd held them in her lap, she'd closed her eyes and pretended just for a little while they were hers. But there were already sticky spots on the TV screen and her cozy library had become a fort, with blankets spread over upended sofa cushions. Barbie dolls and their attendant paraphernalia were scattered from one end of the room to the other.

She loved it. She knew they would be gone when she

got home; Jessie had told her that when she arrived to baby-sit. Their mother was home from the hospital and anxious to have her little girls back.

It was harder to let children go when she hadn't met the mother, especially when, as in this instance, they were returning to their home. They weren't going to the safety of a shelter or even the more dubious protection of relatives, but back to the arena where their mother had been beaten and chances were good they'd seen it.

Meeting their mother had nothing to do with it, she realized; it was hardest to let them go when she knew with every fiber of her being that someone would have them to stay again. And maybe the next time, the bruises and cuts would be on the children instead of the mom.

"Do you want some coffee?" she asked, when Micah parked in front of her garage door. "Or some wine?"

"Sure."

He held her hand as they walked to the house, then took the key from her and unlocked the door, and Landy allowed herself to enjoy the small gestures of being in a relationship. He walked a little ahead of her through the darkened hallway to the kitchen, and she saw his head move as he made sure all was safe.

"Let's sit on the porch," she suggested. "The nights are too nice to stay inside."

When the coffee was brewed and they were settled on the porch swing, he said, "You mentioned once that you took the realty course during a 'time in your life.' When was that?"

"While I was married to Blake. He didn't want me

to work outside and I was going crazy staying home. I didn't want to sit on boards and go to luncheons the way my grandmother did, so I took classes. I not only learned realty, I also learned first aid, how to quilt, embroider and cross-stitch, decorate cakes and make baskets. I took computer classes and an upholstery class. I got my elementary and secondary education teaching licenses." She laughed, remembering. "It was suggested that I leave the upholstery class. I hurt myself so often they were worried about liability."

"What did you like best?"

"Everything that didn't involve math or science. I still quilt and embroider, and have given so many wall-hangings as gifts that people run when they see me coming with a wrapped present."

She thought of the Sunbonnet Sue quilt upstairs in her room, the one that she wanted to be finished but never would, and even considered showing it to him. She dismissed the thought immediately. Showing it to him would require that she explain about the Railroad.

Here was something else that made her feel lonely, she realized. Even when Micah was with her, his fingers laced with hers and his leg bumping hers on the porch swing, trust took a holiday. She was afraid to let him know about her "guests" and he shared only the most superficial parts of his life with her.

She lifted her head to look at him and allowed her eyes to drift closed when his lips lowered to hers. When he released her hand and gathered her to him, she went willingly, tunneling her hands through his hair and thrilling to the beat of his heart. Steady and strong and as much a part of the night as the sound of crickets from the river below them. His scent blended with that of lilacs and the earthy aroma of the river in spring, and she dropped her hands to his shoulders, wanting to be even closer.

"I would love," he said after a while, "to go inside with you. I'd like to take you upstairs to that roomful of roses and make love with you till sunrise. But we're not ready for that, are we, Landy?"

She shook her head. "No." And even though she couldn't trust Micah, the reporter, she owed truth to Micah, the man. "And I don't know if I'll ever be." She met his eyes in the shimmery light from the River Walk.

His fingers rested on the thigh of her bad leg, and she laid her hand on his. "This leg isn't the only damage," she continued. "I'm not able to…respond like a woman normally would. I like foreplay and I like what comes after," she admitted, "but I don't like the middle part. It's not that I'm afraid—that's one thing I'm actually not scared of—but I just can't respond."

He nodded, his chin rubbing the top of her head with the movement. "Did you ever have sex with anyone but Blake?"

She'd told him the truth; that didn't mean she wanted to discuss it further. "No," she said, almost childishly, "And I don't want to."

His sigh was so slight she felt it rather than heard it. "Okay," he said quietly. "I have no intention of forcing you into doing anything you don't want to."

She felt immediate remorse. "I know that. I do." She turned her head to meet his eyes again, their foreheads bumping. "I like you so much," she whispered. "I don't want to alienate you with my neuroses."

His kiss was almost tentative in its gentleness. "Oh, Miss Scarlett, darlin', I don't alienate so easily."

"Promise?"

"Uh-huh."

They sat back, drinking their coffee and making desultory conversation. A half hour later, he left her at her door after a breath-stealing kiss that left her knees trembling.

She went up the stairs slowly, her leg tired and aching. At the door of her bedroom, she looked inside, seeing the wallpaper, the lacy curtains, the quilt she'd made after her divorce when life was full of hope. The bed was an antique she'd found in the attic of her grandmother's house. Solid cherry, its headboard nearly reached the ceiling and the mattress was high enough she had to hoist herself into bed or use the little cherry step that slid underneath.

Looking at the bed, she could easily imagine Micah in it, his tousled head and strong back leaning against the shining wood. She saw him bare-chested and with his legs showing between the folds of tangled sheets, even though she'd never so much as seen him without a shirt.

But she wanted to. She wanted to see that naked chest, feel his skin against her skin, smell his scent as it mingled with hers, and taste both his mouth and the saltiness where his skin grew damp.

The thoughts made her thighs grow weak as moisture built between them, and she leaned against the door frame. Her reflection gazed back at her from the cheval mirror across the room, seeming to mock her, and she frowned. "All you need is a cat and a ball bat under the bed," she said aloud, "and you'll be one of those frightened spinsters who get killed in thrillers."

She stepped into the room and began to undress. In the bathroom, she washed off her makeup and creamed her skin, stroking up and out the way she'd learned in a cosmetology class she'd taken years ago.

Tears welled so suddenly she couldn't stop them, dropping off her lower lids to make rivulets in the unabsorbed cream on her cheeks.

Classes. She'd taken all the ones she'd listed to Micah and more, but none of them had taught her how to trust, how to share her body or what was in her heart. They'd shown her how to care for a classroom full of students, her skin, her home and her furniture, but not how to maintain a relationship with someone she loved.

She remembered the time she'd used "simmering rage" in creative writing class and the instructor had drawn a dark red line through it. He said it turned her prose from the flowery side of lavender to an unbecoming shade of purple.

He hadn't said that other emotions simmered as well. Fear, hate, love, joy and despair all bubbled below the surface with nowhere to go. What would happen if she let them out? If she admitted loud and clear that sometimes she hated Blake for what he'd done to her, that she feared so many things because past hurts had been so grievous, that despair dogged her every hitching step because she knew in her heart of hearts that Landy Wisdom would never be whole?

And what about the love and the joy? They were things she allowed herself in small doses; she loved Jessie and Eli and their families, she felt joy in being around them. And there were feelings for Micah that waved through her at unexpected and sparkling times, feelings that had to do with love and joy.

But fear was stronger, and despair won over all.

Chapter Seven

Window Over the Sink, Taft Tribune: *Sometimes, no matter what you do, the day just stinks.*

Micah felt like he was back in high school and going steady, although that was something he hadn't done then. Almost every night, he went to Landy's house or she came to his. They ate dinner, washed dishes and sat on the porch and talked. Sometimes they were joined by Eli and Jessie, sometimes by Ethan and Nancy, but more often they were alone. A couple of times they went to the movies, eating supper Down at Jenny's before the seven o'clock show, stopping again afterward for coffee.

He umpired more softball games and, when Joe

Carter asked him, some Little League games as well. He didn't like it—the fallen faces of very young batters made him feel like Ebenezer Scrooge after a visit from the ghost of Christmas Present—but Nancy's talk of trust had gotten under his skin.

Allison Scott had come back to work, pale and tired, but insisting her mother was on the mend. Her first day back, Micah gave her assignments, asked her if she had any special projects she wanted to work on, then took her to lunch at Jenny's. In the five years he'd worked with Allie, he'd never taken her out for a meal, although they'd had more than a few beers together in bars across from courthouses.

Over blueberry pie with ice cream, he asked her if there was anything he could do to help regarding her mother's illness. Was she doing okay with child care? Did she need to take some vacation or even a leave of absence? He knew someone who did yard work without charging an arm and a leg if she…

He'd looked up, certain he was making a fool of himself with all this uncustomary personal concern. Allison was crying silently, her small, pointy face awash in tears. He gave her his handkerchief, signaled the waitress for more coffee and stared across the table with horror mixed with compassion. Reporters didn't *cry.* Not in public. Oh, sure, they wanted to, and when they got home they did; they cried and drank and railed against life's iniquities. But not while they sat in cafés eating blueberry pie a la mode with their bosses. Never then.

"Allie?" he said. "What's going on?"

"Nothing." She blew her nose and waved a hand. "I'm just tired, is all."

"Do you need more time off? We'll survive for a few more days if you—"

"No." She smiled, albeit blearily. "I'll be fine."

Back at the office, he glowered at the receptionist. "This trust and caring and being involved business is for the birds." He gathered a notebook from his desk and cadged a couple of pens from the cracked mug beside her phone. "I'm going to go see if anything's going on at the Rotary meeting, then I'm going over to Landy's. She'll be normal." Ignoring Nancy's grin, he left the office again.

After a non-eventful Rotary Club meeting, he found Landy in her den. She was sewing something on a hoop in her lap, which she stuffed behind a cushion when he walked into the room. She was also eating ice cream from its round carton and watching "American Movie Classics" on television. Micah looked at the screen and saw Jimmy Stewart and Maureen O'Hara.

Oh, hell, he couldn't compete with Jimmy Stewart, or even with the kind of ice cream that cost five bucks a quart.

This entire day was looking to be a mistake.

"I rang the bell," he said, when she gave him an accusing look.

"I didn't answer," she said succinctly, "because I didn't want to see anyone. My leg hurts, my hair is dirty and the ice cream is all gone. I do not need any more grief."

He picked up the wineglass at her elbow. "Would you like some more of this?"

She nodded, barely, and he took the spindly glass to the kitchen to refill it, thinking a Mason jar might be a better receptacle in her present frame of mind. He got himself a beer, too, even though she hadn't offered it. The phone rang and he looked over at where the cordless normally hung on the wall near the door. She must have the receiver with her.

It was at her ear when he went back into the den. She nodded thanks when he set down her glass, then turned her head in a way that told him she wanted privacy.

Feeling offended and unsure why, since he tended to be a private person himself, he took his beer to the back porch and sat in the swing with his foot on the rail. At least out here, there was no one to burst into tears or give him dirty looks out of secretive eyes.

There it was. That was what offended him, not her need for privacy. It was that furtive look she got, like he was going to expose every moldy skeleton she had in her closet if he got a sniff inside the door. He was doing his level best to prove that he wasn't a predatory son of a bitch, which was how Allison referred to over-zealous members of their shared profession. He'd been nice to everyone's kids, shown concern for his employees and had even kissed Colby Whatshisname's bald little head when he was rocking him in church.

And when Landy had told Micah the one-year-old

baby was bald because of chemotherapy, he'd gone home and sat and stared at the River Walk until he'd gained enough control to call Colby's parents and ask if there was anything the *Taft Tribune* could do to ease their situation.

The phone call had resulted in the best story he'd written since returning to Taft, a fish fry benefit scheduled at the church, and a talent show that had brought in enough money to keep Colby's parents from losing their house while they fought to keep from losing their son.

It had all, Micah admitted, made him feel good. At least till he went back to church and kissed Colby's shiny little head. After that, he didn't think he'd ever feel good again unless the boy was completely cured.

"I'm sorry."

Landy's voice came softly above the sound of the back door opening and closing. She walked over to sit beside him, her limp more pronounced than usual, and he reached for the hand that lay in her lap, holding it against his own leg as if to give her strength in hers.

"Bad day?" he asked, his anger lost in the lines of pain that radiated from her eyes and mouth.

She nodded, not looking at him. Her eyes were focused on the river, wending its idle way toward the Ohio. "Micah, have you ever hit a woman?"

"No," he said shortly. He didn't like it that she'd felt the need to ask. "Nor do I kick dogs, abuse cats or torture small children. I've had all my shots, make decent money and don't drink to excess. Do I pass?"

Her look was reproachful. "That's not why I asked.

I just wondered if you'd ever been tempted, if a woman had ever driven you to even consider smacking her one."

"I don't think so." He shook his head and gave the swing a slight push with his foot. "I've been mad enough that I've hit other things—I learned how to patch drywall when I was in high school because I put my fist through a wall. In college, a guy got going on how country boys were only good for shooting hoops and running up and down the football field and I got pissed off and smacked a desk. Broke a bone in my hand, but it saved that little jerk's face. I outweighed him by fifty pounds," he added honestly. "If he'd been bigger, I'd probably have hit him." He looked at her, the pallor in her cheeks making him frown. "Why do you ask?"

"Today's Blake's birthday," she said. "I've thought about him a lot, and there's a part of me that's always going to wonder what I could have done differently."

Her gaze was still far away, and he followed it with his own and saw Lucas Trent on the other side of the river, meandering up the Walk with his head down, his hands buried in his pockets. Against his will, Micah felt pity stir inside him for the man who'd lost his only child, who had felt the same way bald little Colby's parents felt.

"I know how much losing Blake hurt him and that he still blames me, but I miss Lucas. He was like my own father."

"To stop blaming you would mean he'd have to accept part of the responsibility."

She looked at him. "What do you mean?"

"Blake's violence wasn't confined to his wives, Landy. He was violent on the football field, too. Even before that, when we were kids and would get into tussles, he always aimed to hurt, never to subdue. Lucas knows that—on some level, he probably knew it then. But as long as he blames everything on you, he doesn't have to go back to when Blake was a kid, and the bad behavior went unchecked."

"I never thought of it that way." She watched Lucas for a moment, her expression sad. "I feel sorry for him. Sometimes when I see him, I think he misses me, too. Or maybe I just want to believe he does."

"Well." He stretched, putting his arm around her and holding her close. "I think you should feel sorry for me. I brought you wine and tried to be an understanding kind of guy and you haven't even kissed me hello."

She grinned at him. "I never kiss you hello."

"I know, and I've been meaning to talk to you about that."

"I can't start now, anyway. My hair's dirty."

He gasped. "Heaven forbid I be kissed by a woman with dirty hair."

"If you'll go home now," she bargained, "I'll wash my hair and come over and cook dinner. How would that be?"

"I can do better than that. If you get your hair really clean, you can come over and *I'll* cook dinner."

She waved a hand airily. "If you insist."

It wasn't until he was parking the Blazer in his garage that Micah realized he'd been finessed into cooking dinner. He was grinning ruefully at himself in the rear view mirror when something else occurred to him.

Landy had been trying to get rid of him.

"You'll be safe here."

Landy had said the words way too many times before, but situations like this one made her more uneasy than usual. The little girls she knew only as Britt and Andie were back, even though the Railroad tried to avoid visitors returning to the same place, and this time their mother was with them. The young woman's haunted eyes and bruised face seemed familiar, as did the way she favored her right arm.

It was how Landy knew she had looked once upon a time, and the knowledge made her queasy. It always did.

But there was something else in the familiarity. In spite of the no-last-names policy of Safe Harbor Railroad, the rule she'd never considered bending, much less breaking, she said, "I know you, don't I?"

"Yes." The woman lifted her head, meeting her gaze with an intense blue one. There were marks—hand-prints—on her neck.

Landy shuddered inwardly, remembering the young reporter who'd helped her that long-ago day. "I never had the chance to thank you."

Her guest shrugged. "You're more than compensating with what you're doing now. The girls have talked of nothing but you and your pretty house since… since…" Her voice faded away.

"Since last time." Landy let the words ring out, so harsh they seemed to scrape the air. *Don't tell me he didn't mean to, that it won't happen again, that it was probably your fault. Don't do it.*

"Yes, since last time." Landy poured tea from the pot and set a cup in front of her guest, then took glasses of chocolate milk into the den where Britt and Andie had already erected a fort and were sitting inside it watching television.

When she came back to the kitchen, she sat across from the woman, her cup warming her hands.

Resentment shone from the brilliant blue eyes across the table. "We don't all have a big house to run to or a trust fund to live on. Some of us have to support our families and you can't do that when you're on the run." She tossed her head, the gesture causing pain to flutter over her sharp features. "We can't all kill our abusers and get away with it."

The attack took Landy's breath as certainly as if it had been physical. "Is that what you think?" she said. "That I've gotten away with something."

Landy held the other woman's gaze until the blue eyes looked away, regret replacing the resentment in her guest's expression. "Of course not," the woman said stiffly. "I'm sorry."

Landy supposed it had been only a matter of time until one of her guests was someone she knew. Taft was a small town, and although Eli's territory covered the entire township, the population was small.

Often, however, hers was the second depot on the

guest's journey to a shelter, sometimes even the third. Although it was wearing for the women and children being shuttled from place to place, bitter experience had taught the administrators of Safe Harbor Railroad that a long, winding underground trail was safest for the travelers.

She had been taking in guests since shortly after settling into the little bungalow, longer than was advised by the administrators. "Regardless of the secrecy and the anonymity, someone knows, or someone will find out, that you're harboring people who have run away from their families. When they find out, you're in danger, and the longer you do it, the more dangerous it gets."

Eli's words had been serious the first time he said them, warning the second, angry the third and last. But he was still a conductor on Safe Harbor Railroad, more exposed to danger than she, so she didn't listen to him.

Sometimes she was afraid. She would lie awake as the accustomed sounds of the river and the trees on the Walk grew sinister and threatening to her ear. When children were involved, she was furious, the anger especially frustrating because there was nowhere to direct it.

She worked on the quilt then; stitching a square for every guest. The boys on the quilt were in straw hats, girls in sunbonnets, women in dipping picture hats. Black hatbands were appliquéd on a few squares. Landy and Jessie always sewed them together, their mouths held tight against the hurt of it, and they cried for the people they'd lost, who wouldn't be wounded in the name of love ever again.

Today, when the new yet familiar visitor lashed out at her, she'd been hurt. She wanted to go up to bed and squirrel in with her quilt squares. Then they'd be sorry.

The realization that she had no idea who "they" were made her grin in spite of her blue mood.

At least, at the end of this crummy, crummy day, she was going to spend time with Micah. Eat the dinner he cooked and wash dishes with his hip bumping against hers and watch the moon rise over the Twilight.

Maybe, since her hair was clean, she'd kiss him hello.

Chapter Eight

Window Over the Sink, Taft Tribune: *Back in what my kids consider the Dark Ages of rock and roll, Don and Phil Everly had a hit called "Love Hurts." Others have recorded it since, but when I think of it, I think of the perfect vocal harmony of the Everly Brothers. Perfect harmony, you know, is at odds with the way the song of love actually goes.*

"Why am I doing this?" Micah muttered, dropping a spoonful of applesauce on a plate with a slight splat.

"As I recall, it was your idea." Eli put two pieces of fish onto another plate and handed it to Micah.

"My idea was a nice, small fish fry in the church basement, not a free for all in the park."

"Then you shouldn't have printed up so many tickets. Every one of them sold, and more people are paying when they get here." Eli turned slightly to address someone behind them. "We need more bread, please, and Micah's almost out of applesauce."

Micah felt something around his leg and looked down into Colby's shining face. "Hey, buddy." He lifted the baby and held him on his hip. "So what do you think?" he said. "You think we'll make enough money tonight to get you some hair?"

"Micah, you do realize you can't buy his health, don't you?" said Eli. He stepped aside for Jessie to dump more fish into the pan he was serving from, but his gaze remained fastened on Micah.

"I know that." Micah rubbed noses with Colby before handing him to his mother and looking up at the line of people waiting for food. "Whoa, slumming, are we?" He kept his voice low.

"What are you—good evening, Mr. Trent. Nice to see you here. Two pieces or three?" Eli didn't stutter, nor did his welcoming smile fade.

"Two, thank you." Lucas Trent was polite, even nodding to Micah as he proceeded through the line.

"Daddy?" Wendy appeared between her father and Micah. "Hi, Uncle Mike. Excuse me." She stood on tiptoe to whisper to her father.

Micah saw his eyes widen, then he gave his daughter a one-armed hug. "The Lord works in mysterious ways."

When Wendy had darted away through the crowd of people, Micah gave Eli a questioning look.

"Lucas didn't have a ticket," said Eli in a low voice, "so he dropped his cash donation into the big pickle jar like everyone else did. The money was folded, and Wendy and Hannah thought he'd put in a ten or a few singles, but he didn't. It was five one-hundred-dollar bills."

Micah looked over at where the attorney sat alone at the end of a table and felt that unwilling pity again. As he watched, Landy passed her former father-in-law with a pitcher of punch. When she would have gone on with only a nod, Trent said something to her, and she turned to look at him, her head bent slightly as she listened.

"Jessie." Micah spoke over his shoulder.

"You need more already?" She approached with a can of applesauce. Her gaze lifted, following his. She set down the can and took the spoon from his hand. "Go."

He sifted through the crowd, scarcely aware when Lindsey joined him, capturing his hand and trotting to keep up with his long stride.

"Landy." He reached her, and snagged her waist with his free arm. "People are waiting for refills. What kind of waitress are you?"

"One who works cheap," she said immediately. "Linds, you going to help me?" She dipped her head toward Trent. "It was nice of you to come, Lucas."

She walked away, an extra little bounce in her hitching step, with Lindsey ahead of her saying in her piping voice, "D'you want some more of this red junk?"

"You can call off the cavalry, Walker," said Trent dryly. "I come in peace. Your father says there's no fool like an old fool, says even if Landis was ever guilty of anything—which he gravely doubts—she's suffered enough for two lifetimes." Sorrow and something like hope flickered across his features. "Perhaps he's right."

"You mean we finally get to eat?" Landy looked with pleasure and a growling stomach at the covered plates Jessie set on the table on Eli's back verandah.

Micah poured wine into glasses. "Is this left over from the last communion Sunday, Eli?"

"Nope." Eli brought a cheesecake to the table and set it in the center. "We use grape juice. This is from your rack. I ran in there on the way home and swiped it from right under your father's nose." He lifted the bottle and regarded the label with an appreciative sigh. "I don't think even the Catholics get to use stuff this good. Of course, it's probably better because I stole it."

"Was Nancy there? At my house, I mean, when you cadged the wine?" asked Micah when they were all seated.

"Uh-huh." Eli leered. "She was…er…right under your dad's nose, too. That might have had something to do with why he didn't answer when I yelled, 'Hi, Ethan, I'm stealing some wine.'"

Jessie frowned at him. "It's not at all godly to gossip, nor is it becoming to someone in your position."

Eli gasped. "Samson's shorn sideburns, you don't

say! You should be in the pulpit, Jess, what with that gift you have for pontificating."

"It's all right," said Micah. "Pop gossips about us all the time. That's just the way it is in a small town. He talks about Eli in particular."

"Oh, that's true," said Landy. "It's just awful."

Jessie's expression changed from mutinous to interested. Eli looked resigned.

"There was discussion just the other day," Landy went on, "about Eli's hair. Does he dye it? Is it really his?"

"I hope you set them straight," said Eli righteously.

"We did." Micah beamed at him. "I said it was yours because you'd paid for it and Landy said she didn't really consider highlighting hair the same as dying it."

"Thank you so much. It's good to know I can count on my friends." Eli dipped his head in grave recognition of their support.

"Speaking of gossip," said Jessie, "what did Lucas have to say to you at the fish fry, Landy? I thought Micah was going to break a leg getting over to you."

Landy thought back to the moment when Lucas had said her name. She'd thought she was going to drop her pitcher of juice. "He said my lilacs had been beautiful this year, then he asked how my roses were coming along and recommended some new food for them." She shrugged, pleasure flowing through the motion. "That was about it."

"Pop says he's changing." Micah looked at Landy. *What do you think? Do you think people can change?*

Landy served the cheesecake, reserving judgment on the questions in his eyes. Today's conversation aside, memory was sharp of Lucas Trent in the courtroom, staring at her through eyes unnervingly like Blake's had been. The recollection of reporters swarming her yard like angry bees was strong, as well, and she gripped her hands together in her lap for a moment, willing away the melancholy the memories evoked.

She watched Micah as they ate their dessert, feeling her heart respond more and more to the man who'd dished out seven hundred servings of applesauce because he wanted to help a child.

She sat still, barely listening to the conversation that flowed around her. They were talking about trains, recalling when the whistle of the C & O had punctuated most conversations in Taft. The sheriff used to say that speeding wasn't a problem in Taft because there were so many railroad crossings it slowed everybody down.

"I remember my dad sitting and cussing the trains while we waited," said Eli. "I learned some of my best swear words that way, and now it's all gone to waste."

"I did a story on the C & O while I was in Lexington," said Micah, "and it brought back all kinds of memories, but I left out the cuss words." He pushed his plate away, "Speaking of trains, do any of you know anything about the Safe Harbor Railroad?"

Landy felt the color draining from her face as she returned to earth with a bump that was so hard it felt physical, twinging through her bad leg in a coil of pain. Eli said casually, "Where did you hear about that?"

Micah shrugged. "A reporter mentioned it when I first came back here and then again later. Plus I heard little pieces and parts about it in relationship to other things."

What had she been thinking? If he hadn't talked about his work with her, it was because he was waiting, gathering information before going in for the kill. What an exposé that would make. She wondered almost hysterically what angle Micah would take and how she would fit into the story. Would she be the battered ex-wife who killed her abuser in a fit of rage? A vigilante who hated all men? A pathetic figure who lived crippled and alone rather than make a new life for herself?

She met his eyes and marveled that they could appear so guileless. Had he known about the Railroad all along? Had she really been the debutante he remembered with affection or just a potential source of information?

"I'm not feeling very well," she said, looking away from Micah's curious gaze. "Eli, do you mind if I don't help with the dishes?" She got to her feet clumsily, grasping the white-painted arm of her chair for support.

"I'll take you," said Micah.

"I'd rather walk." She made a vague gesture of dismissal. "It might clear my head."

Jessie came around the table, grasping her elbows and looking into her eyes. "Do you want me to come over?"

"Leave Eli here with nine kids? Are you crazy?" Landy gave her friend a hug. "I'll call you tomorrow."

Micah walked her home as she'd known he would. To have allowed her to go alone wouldn't fit into his "good guy" persona, the image he'd cultivated since his return to Taft.

Resentment and hurt almost choked her. When he took her hand, she drew it away with a mute shake of her head. "I don't want to talk," she said succinctly, "and I don't need help walking."

"Really? And to what do I owe this sudden trip into the deep freeze?" He stayed at her side, close enough that the hair on his arms brushed her skin, and suddenly she hated her infirmity with a new passion.

"Let me think." His voice was light, that deceptive kind of airiness that hid banked anger, and Landy forced herself not to shrink away. "We had dessert. Did I eat too much or not enough or simply use a wrong fork? Did I drink too much wine? Maybe you just don't like talking about trains. How *does* one piss off a debutante?"

"Stop it!" She moved away, sitting on a park bench and drawing her knees up beneath her chin, ignoring the muscles that screamed in her leg.

"Come on, Landy, give me a clue." He hunkered down in front of her, propping his elbows on his knees. "We're too old for this kind of game-playing."

She glared at him. "You're a good one to talk about playing games, aren't you? Running around pretending to be Mr. Nice Guy when you're not nice at all, just a reporter on the lookout for a story."

* * *

The conversation went downhill from there. Landy closed her back door in his face with a curt "good-night," and Micah walked home to sit on his porch and stare moodily at the river. The Twilight had no answers for his silent questions; it just lapped against the shore, the soft slapping sound offering none of the peace it usually did.

Ethan joined him, handing him a cup of coffee and taking a seat.

"Mom ever get mad at you for no good reason that you could figure out?" asked Micah, feeling like an adolescent.

His father snorted. "All the time."

"What did you do?"

He looked away from the river in time to see a look of longing cross Ethan's face. Micah averted his gaze, unable to bear the bittersweet pain of his father's loss.

"Grovel."

"Huh?" The answer was so unexpected that Micah let his feet drop from the porch railing in surprise. Ethan was what had once been called a "man's man." He drank his coffee black, his whiskey neat and his beer direct from the bottle. He had been the breadwinner of Micah's child-hood, and his wife the homemaker, a twain that had never met.

Ethan Walker wouldn't grovel.

Would he?

"It took me the better part of twenty years to figure

that out," said Ethan. "Sometimes I had done something, and sometimes I hadn't, but it was better to grovel a bit till I got to the bottom of whatever the trouble was."

"Better for whom?"

"Both of us. If she was hurt, she needed to know I was sorry. That stuff in *Love Story* about love meaning you never have to say you're sorry might be okay for some people, but not anyone I ever knew. If you blew it, you need to apologize. If you didn't, well, that'll all come out in the wash."

Ethan got to his feet. "I'm for bed." He pressed Micah's shoulder as he walked past.

Micah went back to staring at the river, sipping coffee that had gone cold. *What had set her off?* The fish fry had been a resounding success. The conversation among the four of them at dinner had been fun and stimulating. Even Lucas Trent's involvement in the day had been unexpectedly positive.

Did she really not like talking about trains?

He frowned into his cup, trying to remember if Eli and Jessie had responded to what he'd considered an innocent question. They hadn't answered—the question had been lost in his and Landy's departure—but he didn't think they'd been angry, either.

Certain he wouldn't be able to sleep, he went inside and booted up his laptop. Nothing wrong with getting a jump on writing his column. He'd finished the last one about three minutes before deadline.

He thought about the Safe Harbor Railroad. He knew the bare bones of what it was, and when he'd worked in Lexington, he'd probably have done a story on it. Not an exposé, but a human interest piece. He wouldn't have used real names or locations, but someone would have figured it out.

In Taft, it didn't occur to him to either write or assign the story; too many people would be hurt. But Landy didn't know that about him. The fact made him a little angry, because he thought she *should* have known it by now.

The blank computer screen mocked him, and he clicked the cursor on the *X* in the corner and closed the program. He stared at the computer until the screen-saver came on. The flying windows made him think of Susan Billings' column, and he frowned into the darkness outside the window.

She was right. Love was a real bitch.

Chapter Nine

Window Over the Sink, Taft Tribune: *Of all the things I like about living in a small town, the biggest is the absence of fear. We know bad things happen, and we're fully cognizant that they could happen to us, but we do not allow fear to rule us. It is a comfortable thing.*

"We'll leave tonight," said Allison. Her bruises, at least the ones that showed, were healing. They were the sickly yellow that was fairly easy to disguise with full-coverage makeup.

"All right." Landy sat across the table from her. "What do you want to do? Is your job in jeopardy?"

"I don't think so. He's a good boss."

He. Him. His. That's how they referred to Micah. It meant neither of them had to acknowledge the other's relationship to him.

Allie turned her cup in circles on its saucer, picked it up, set it down. "He's the only person I ever worked for who didn't always put the story first."

"Really?" Landy tried to sound disinterested. It didn't work very well; her voice went up and down like an old-fashioned pump handle.

"Why do you think there hasn't been a story on the Safe Harbor Railroad?"

"Because he doesn't know what it is." *Why else?*

"Sure, he does. He said to let him know if there was anything the paper could do to help the Railroad, and he's asked questions about it. Being an editor hasn't done anything to lessen his reporter's curiosity. But he's never suggested that we do even the breath of a story."

Landy wanted to believe her. If only Micah hadn't asked that question the night before. Why would he have asked if he already knew the answers? Unless he was digging for more. Or unless he really was just curious.

The timer went off and she got up to take cookies out of the oven. "Did you mention any names when you talked to him about it?"

"I didn't know any." Allie peeled potatoes carefully.

She did everything *very* carefully, Landy had noticed, and remembered going through the same motions herself. If she did everything right, she'd reasoned, Blake wouldn't have anything to be angry about. It had taken years for her to realize he didn't need a reason.

"How did it happen?" she asked, even though she never asked guests that question. She knew how it happened.

Allie shrugged, wincing when the motion jarred her arm. "We were out and I met a guy I'd been in journalism school with. My husband was friendly to him, suggested having dinner with him and his girlfriend sometime, the whole nine yards. Then, when we got home, Jason went apeshit. I blamed it on booze, him being tired, being laid off from his job, anything I could blame it on."

"That explains the first time," said Landy. "What about after that?"

"He says he'll kill himself if I leave him," said Allie. She looked up and met Landy's eyes. "And he says he'll kill me before he lets me go."

They met on the River Walk just after dawn, falling into step together. Silence stretched between them.

"I don't like it when you sound like a reporter," said Landy finally. "Asking questions and looking suspicious. You know Taft as well as anyone, and that we like privacy."

"I *am* a reporter," Micah said mildly, "and I don't mean to look suspicious. I wasn't even aware I did."

"I know I'm being childish." She sat down on a bench with a sigh, her leg hurting too much to keep up a pretense that everything was fine, just fine.

He sat beside her, not touching her, his legs stretched out in front of him. "Tell me about it."

Landy thought it might be nice to have friends who let her crawl into a hole and cover her head. She didn't like talking about that time; it was like reliving it.

"They were there every day when I came home from the courthouse," she said, tossing him a resentful look. "Vans would fill the driveway so I had to walk to the house from the street, crutches and all, and it was like going through a maze. They'd leave litter all over the yard cups and sandwich wrappers and such. I'd pick it up and the next day it would be back again. One reporter even referred to 'the defendant's cluttered lawn' in a story."

"Were they all like that?"

"No, not all." She stopped and met his gaze and it was as though she heard her story through his ears. "Actually, there were only a few, but they made me so miserable I blamed them all. And there was even a woman, who helped me when I fell." She couldn't tell him it was Allison, she reminded herself, because the story wasn't hers to tell.

"Other than the reporters' rudeness and their mess, how were the stories themselves?" Micah offered her a mint from the roll in his pocket.

Landy sucked on the peppermint and gave herself a moment to think about the shape of his mouth and the pleasure of kissing him before answering. "I didn't read them. Jessie did—she even kept them. That's how I knew about the reference to my yard. According to her, they were accurate for the most part."

She felt her anger leaving her, being lulled away by peppermint and the curve of his lips and the warmth of his leg next to hers on the bench. In an effort to hold onto it, she said, "Why did you ask us about Safe Harbor?"

His smile was endearingly lopsided, and his touch light when he fingered a tendril of her hair. "Because I know and care for someone who could have used it a few years ago."

She returned his smile and the touch, tracing her finger down the hard length of his jaw. "I would have had to decide I needed it, and I'm not sure I ever reached that point. I thought I'd solved all my problems by getting a divorce."

"Before that, before you finally walked away, didn't anyone ever—I don't know, stage an intervention or something?"

"Good heavens, you don't think anyone knew, do you? Eli wasn't here then, and even though Jessie had a real strong inkling, she wasn't sure. Plus she had problems of her own." She adopted a haughty air. "Debutantes don't *tell,* you know. Someone might decide they're only human."

He grinned at her, and she thought maybe she could live with seeing his face every day for the rest of her life. Unsettled by the notion, she pushed herself to her feet, stifling a groan when her leg raged at her. "I need to get moving or I'll never make it to church."

"Want a ride? I'll buy lunch afterward."

Landy hesitated. It would be another step in their relationship. Going to church together in Taft was almost like being engaged.

"All right."

He slipped his arm around her waist when they reached the path to her house. "There was another reason I asked about Safe Harbor."

"What was that?" she asked warily.

"I know somebody," he said, "who 'visits her sick mother' a lot—but always comes back covered with bruises…"

Chapter Ten

Window Over the Sink, Taft Tribune: *Sometimes I look at my children and marvel at the breadth and depth of the love I feel for them. I asked my mother the other day when I would stop looking at the kids and saying, "Isn't it amazing?" She said she'd let me know.*

"You don't have to fix my walk. I can hire someone to do it." Landy glared down at the top of Micah's head. The sun lit little gold flames in his dark brown hair. Delicious. She sighed.

"Yeah, right, then I'd have to hire someone to hang the border in my bathroom and we'd both end up broke."

"You could probably manage that yourself."

He looked up from where he knelt beside her sidewalk. "But I don't want to. You look nice. Going somewhere?"

"A meeting."

She didn't elaborate, and he looked up again. "The Railroad?"

"Uh-huh."

"Why does that make you unhappy?"

"It doesn't."

"It does so. You've got that look the girls get when I call them out at softball games, the one that always makes me feel bad." He straightened on crackling knees and dropped a light kiss on her mouth.

"Why does it make you feel bad?" she asked.

"Because I'd like for them all to be safe at home."

She smiled at him. "Me, too." Then she sighed. "I think I'm mad because Nancy and your dad are coming to the meeting...with Lucas. I'm not so worried about your dad, but Lucas is another story."

"Ethan asked if he could come and bring Lucas. When I wondered what their interest was and what Lucas's motives were, Ethan just said he shouldn't have to tell a preacher about atonement." Eli spoke softly, looking over his shoulder to see who entered the meeting room.

"What if it's all a ruse and he exposes us?" Landy asked. "A lot of people know the Safe Harbor Railroad exists, but no one is ever named. What if Lucas tells all, or Ethan lets something slip to Micah and Micah runs with it? What then, Eli?"

"Then we'll deal with it. Exposure has always been a risk. You're as aware of that as anyone. How long have we been trying to get you to stop being a depot?"

"For a long time," she acknowledged. "But I don't have anything to lose, Eli. You do. Jessie does." She nodded in the direction of the few others who staffed the Railroad. "So do some of them."

"And every time somebody new came in, we worried about exposure." Eli got up, as Nancy, Ethan and Lucas entered the room. "It's time."

Railroad meetings weren't social events. The items on the agenda were deadly serious, and the very act of discussing them exhausted the members. The newcomers asked questions, but were accepting of the often less-than-satisfactory answers the Railroad had to offer. They dispersed at the end with waves and quiet promises to "see you later." There was no social hour over pie and coffee, no plans made for lunch Down at Jenny's or golf after work the next day.

Landy had her hand on the door handle of her car when Lucas spoke from somewhere behind her. "Landis?"

She turned toward the sound of his voice. "Yes?"

He approached, and she had to stop herself from shrinking from the mere size of him. Standing under the security lights in the church parking lot, his resemblance to his dead son was both eerie and alarming.

Though he wasn't smiling, he wore an apologetic expression with hope lifting the corners of his mouth, and for a moment she saw the Blake she had loved. The memory held her still.

"Could I bother you for a ride home? I came with Ethan and Nancy, and they're very accommodating, but one does feel rather like a fifth wheel in their presence."

Landy had been single for a long time. She understood that feeling. But— "Of course," she said politely. Surely he wasn't looking for a new way to exact revenge. He wouldn't wrest the wheel from her grip and send them both to their deaths at the bottom of the Twilight as they crossed the bridge. He wouldn't pull out the handgun she knew he carried and shoot her point-blank. Would he?

The ride to the River Walk was mostly silent. He asked if she'd tried new food for her roses and said that it looked like rain. A shame after the sunny day they'd had, and there had been too much rain already this spring. She agreed.

"Just as far as your house," he requested. "I'm on the neighborhood watch tonight. I can start from there as easily as anywhere."

But when she parked her old Chevy in the garage, he made no move to get out of the car. She didn't, either, and they sat there, held captive by aching silence and memories of other times. Finally, she said, "Lucas?"

"I appreciate the tea you leave out when I'm on watch," he said. "It's always splendid."

"You taught me how to make it." In one of those other times, a particularly tender one.

"Yes, well, thank you for leaving it."

"You're welcome."

But still he sat there, staring at the gardening tools on a rack on the garage wall. "You need new lawn rakes."

"I know. I'll get them before the leaves fall. Jake always has a good sale at the hardware in August."

"Yes."

"I need to get inside," she said quietly.

"Of course." He reached for the door handle. Then stopped, staring forward again. When he spoke, the words sounded as though they came dragged through broken glass. "When he died," he said, "I wanted to die, too. The only thing that kept me alive was hating you."

God, Lucas, how do you think I *felt? I killed the only man I'd ever loved. Do you think you're the only one who was hurt?*

She looked over at him, ready to say the words she'd only thought, but they died in her throat. She'd cared for this man once. They'd shared cups of tea and long conversations. He'd taught her how to grow roses and she'd chosen the colors when he'd had his house painted. They'd daydreamed together about the children Landy and Blake would have, squabbling laughingly over the name of their firstborn. What was wrong, he had demanded, with a girl named Lucas?

"Would you like to come in?" she asked quietly. "We can have tea and you can take some with you."

"No, I…" The words faded away. "Yes, thank you. I'd like that."

She didn't know what to say to him. She wasn't going to defend herself anymore, nor was she going to discuss the Railroad with him.

But she could talk about Blake to him as she couldn't to anyone else, because Lucas had loved him as much as she had. That was something no one—not even Jessie—fully understood, that Landy had never stopped loving her husband even though she'd come to fear him, to dread his presence. To cause his death.

Once they settled into the kitchen, she poured boiling water over the tea leaves and snuggled a cozy over the pot. "I still miss him, you know? When I light a fire, I can see him leaning over to do it for me because I had such a time getting it to burn right." She laughed, the sound catching in her throat. "He always told me not to worry about it. It was a guy thing."

Lucas smiled, but it was a sad expression. "Once, after you were divorced, he and I talked about why you wouldn't take him back. He told me he'd 'slapped you around.' I told him that was the very worst kind of cowardice, and he said, 'But that's why my mother left, isn't it? Because you hit her.'"

Landy's hands went still. She looked at him, meeting his eyes. "You didn't. Of course, you didn't."

"No, never. She left because she fell in love with someone else. I was angry and I was hurt, and I probably never discussed it with Blake. I guess I expected him to know. His mother never told him, either, but neither did she tell him I'd hit her. I don't know what made him think it was all right. Maybe it was that I always encouraged him to be a man's man. To be the roughest and toughest at football, the best shot with a gun, what we called the meanest son of a bitch in the valley."

Landy poured their tea and sat across from him at the bar in the kitchen. "I was an enabler because I kept it a secret, you because you didn't want to see what he was doing, his mother because she was never where he needed her to be. But in the end, Lucas—" she met his eyes again, an unswerving gaze "—it was Blake's responsibility, his choice to be violent."

"Do you think so?"

It was there in his face again, that vestige of hope she'd seen when he'd asked her for a ride home. How heavy his burden must have been, all the more so because it was weighted down with his hatred of her.

"I know so," she said, surprised at her own certainty. "It's taken me years to know it, but it's true."

Lucas looked up in surprise when the knock came at the back door, but Landy knew who it was. She almost regretted Micah's arrival. She doubted if Lucas's newfound acceptance extended to the possibility that she might enter into a relationship with someone besides Blake.

"Hi," Micah said when she opened the door. "You okay?" He looked past her to where Lucas sat at the counter, and his eyes were cool.

"We were just talking," she said. "I'm fine."

"I should go anyway," said Lucas stiffly, getting to his feet. "I need to get on watch."

"That's all right," said Micah. "I'm not staying."

"Oh, phooey," said Landy. She wasn't having a testosterone battle right here in her own kitchen, not
anymore. "Neither one of you has to go. Come in,
Micah. Is it raining yet?"

"No." He stepped inside. "I hope it doesn't. It would
wash away all the work I did on your walk."

"Did you put a tarp over it?" asked Lucas, sitting
back down.

"Yeah, but you know how the wind kicks up. You
don't have to make coffee," Micah told Landy when she
reached for the coffeemaker carafe. "I can have what
you're having."

She grinned at him. "It would choke you."

"Probably."

Micah took a seat at the bar while she made the
coffee. "Pop came home from the meeting," he said,
"and told me he'd just gone off and left you there. We
had a little chat about manners, then he and Nancy told
me they really didn't need my presence. I thought I was
a little old to be sent to my room, so I came here
instead."

Lucas chuckled, then looked up at the clock on the
wall. "I'd better get out there." He got up and extended
his hand to Micah. "You've grown into a good man. You
were probably a good boy, too, but I couldn't see it."

"Why can you see it now, Lucas?" asked Landy.
"What has made you change?"

The older man shrugged. He looked uncomfortable,
and Landy could tell that Micah felt sorry for him.

"Life's so short and there's so much pain. I hated that I was causing more of it, both to you and myself, Landy. And your father," he said, smiling crookedly at Micah, "makes one see things in a different light, a better light."

"He does that," Micah agreed, "whether you like it or not."

"I don't really have a good explanation," said Lucas, "either for letting the anger go on for so long or for allowing it to end."

"Well, I do." Landy smiled at him, though she felt her expression wobble. "You missed my tea."

Chapter Eleven

Window Over the Sink, Taft Tribune: *Sometimes the air is so heavy before a storm that it feels like a physical threat. I stay in the house and huddle down against the fear of it, turning on lights to challenge the darkness and playing music loud and courageous.*

"It's great," said Micah, looking up at the new wallpaper border that lined his bathroom ceiling, "although I could have done without you being on a ladder when there's no one in the house."

Landy eyed him from where she sat on top of the stepladder. "Life doesn't stop because of a crippled leg."

He looked like he wanted to argue that point. A frown furrowed his forehead and his eyes looked curiously flat.

"Micah?" She stepped down from the ladder and laid a hand on his sleeve. "Is something wrong?"

"I stopped by the hospital to see Colby." His voice sounded ragged. "How much can one tiny little body bear? How much can his parents endure?"

"His body's tiny," she said gently, "but his spirit's huge. His parents just hang on, I suppose, to their faith and to each other. And maybe they latch on to the tail of their baby's spirit and take strength from it." She slipped her arms around his waist, seeking to comfort.

Micah's response was immediate. He held her close, so close his belt buckle dug into the soft flesh under her ribcage.

She swallowed hard. She could feel his rage against Colby's disease radiating off of him. And she was scared.

Rage was rage. Knowing its source didn't make her fear it less. It was there in the tightness of his embrace and the quick thrumming of his heart against her ear. Her own heartbeat escalated to the point that she no longer felt his. She went from trying to comfort him to wanting to get away before he hurt her again.

No, not again. This was Micah, not Blake. She shook her head to clear it. When she spoke, she made her voice firm in a way she'd mastered with students when she substitute-taught. "Micah, you're holding me too tight."

He withdrew, and she immediately wanted to pull

him close again, a response she couldn't have explained if her life depended on it. "I'm sorry—"

He covered her mouth with his fingers. "I scared you," he said, "not the other way around. If anyone's sorry, it's me."

"But everything scares me," she said bleakly. "It's no way to go through life."

He folded the ladder and hooked it over his arm. "Let's go find some coffee. It's been a long day." He paused, looking around the perimeter of his bathroom. "You've done a great job in here. You're quite handy, for a gorgeous woman."

Gathering her paperhanging tools and following him from the room, she caught sight of herself in his mirror. She wore her painting clothes—an ancient T-shirt and sweatpants with the legs cut off—a bandana over her hair and splotches of paste everywhere. The skin on her legs was nearly as white as the paste except where the scars were, and she hadn't shaved them in a few days. She wasn't wearing makeup. Her eyelashes had seemingly disappeared and a streak of the strawberry jam she'd spooned out of the jar for lunch followed the line of her jaw.

"Where," she asked, "are you keeping this woman?"

He came to stand behind her, meeting her eyes in their shared reflection. "Right there," he said quietly, pointing. "She's the real thing, and I like her."

Along with all her fears, neuroses and other hang-ups, Landy was conscious of the fact that no one ever told her they loved her. Her grandmother hadn't bothered to say it and Blake seldom had, either. As close as she and Jessie were, they relied on their relationship to communicate the affection between them.

Sometimes when she was feeling particularly lonely, she literally ached to hear the words.

But in this moment, with her gaze meshing with his steady gray one, "…I like her" came close enough.

She'd stayed late at Micah's, sharing pizza and talking over coffee about what could be done to help Colby and his family, and it never occurred to Landy to dial 911 when she heard the banging on her door. She was sure if someone wanted to hurt her, they wouldn't knock on the door at 2:47 in the morning; they would come up behind her and hit her on the head with a brick. So she pulled on a robe over her nightshirt and limped down the stairs as quickly as she could. The banging didn't stop until she turned on the porch light and yelled, "Just a minute."

"I'm sorry," said Allie when she opened the door. Her two girls stood next to her on the porch, crying. "I'm so sorry."

Landy hurried them inside, pushing Allison into a chair in front of the fireplace and taking the girls upstairs. When she came back down, Allie was staring into the cold fireplace.

"I'll leave. This isn't safe for you. I know it isn't. But I didn't know where to go. I have no money. I didn't even grab my wallet with my identification and my credit cards in it." She drew in a sobbing breath and continued before Landy could speak. "I couldn't believe I ran out of gas. I've been driving for fifteen years, I've been a reporter for ten, and I've never run out of gas. Never." She got to her feet and stood, swaying. "If I can just leave the kids here for the night, I'll go…somewhere and make arrangements. I can call my mother—no, that's the first place he'd check. But I can—"

"Right now," said Landy quietly, "you can sit back down and I'll make you some hot chocolate. It'll help you sleep." She watched as Allie lowered herself carefully into the chair. "Is anything broken? Do you need to go to the emergency room or for me to call a nurse?"

"No." Allie flinched after she shook her head. "I'm not as bad as last time. But he threatened the children, said if they told, then bad Mommy would be taken away." She covered her face with her hands. "I'm *not* a bad mother. I'm *not!*"

"Of course you're not." Landy kept her voice low and soothing. "Here, drink this."

Allie took the cup. "Thank you." The words were more breathed than said.

Landy looked up, feeling a prickle of apprehension. "Oh, for heaven's sake."

She'd left her blinds open. Seldom since the early days of her marriage to Blake had she done that, when he'd shouted at her for trying to attract the men across the river by standing in the kitchen of Grandmother's house with the lights on and the blinds open.

She remembered that closing them had been a two-edged sword. While the simple act had been one thing he could no longer berate her about, it had also given him all the privacy he needed to beat the hell out of her.

She had stayed with him until she lost count of the beatings. There were times when she went to the safe in the library and got the handgun he'd taught her to use. She would take it to the kitchen and clean it carefully and then push the clip into its holder. Occasionally, she chambered a round, flinching at the sound it made as it moved into place. It would be so fast, she thought, and then he could never hurt her again. More than once, God save her, she held the barrel of the gun to her temple.

Oh, but the mess. She couldn't splatter blood and brains all over her grandmother's kitchen, not after all the years Evelyn Titus had spent keeping it spotless.

There would be no heaven, either, for one who took her own life, no possible chance of meeting her parents who'd been killed in a car wreck before their only child's first birthday.

And everyone would feel so sorry for poor, bereaved Blake. If she shut her eyes, she could see him standing beside her closed casket in Halstead's Mortuary, his head bowed in grief as he accepted everyone's condolences.

Some little part of the debutante still lived during those years with Blake, the part of her that was damned if she'd give him that kind of satisfaction. Anger made her unload the gun and put it away. Every single time. By that time, the sun was usually up, lightening the closed blinds, and Landy would open them to face another day.

"Landy?" Allie's voice came softly from behind her. "Are you all right?"

"Yes." She went to the windows, turning the wands that closed the blinds. "Yes, I'm fine now."

He felt like a voyeur, standing at the bottom of her path with his flashlight in his pocket. It was none of his business if she couldn't sleep or if she chose to leave her blinds open.

But she never did, that was all. And she wasn't alone in there. Micah didn't know whether to go up and knock on her door, continue to hide or skulk along home.

His foot slipped on the edge of the path. What if the person in the house with Landy was an unwanted visitor?

He went toward the house, stepping noisily onto the porch. He was part of the neighborhood watch, after all. Wasn't that the purpose, to make sure the neighborhoods were safe? Of course, he'd come off watch a good three hours ago, but safe was safe.

He knocked on the door just as the blinds closed.

Landy's voice came faintly from behind them. "Just a minute."

The door opened without her even asking who would be knocking on it at this time of night.

She wore a robe, her hair was sticking up in soft spikes, and her eyes looked dark and disturbed. "Micah? Are you still on watch?"

"We were playing poker after our shift and Lucas saw your lights. You okay?"

"I'm fine. Just having some trouble sleeping."

"Your leg?"

She made a noncommittal sound, and he felt like yelling, "All right, who's in there?" like some outraged lover. Instead, he said, his voice barely above a whisper, "Is there anything I can do? Do you want me to get Eli or Jessie?"

The look of dismay came and went so quickly he thought he might have imagined it, but then it was replaced by the familiar secretive expression. "No," she said, and looked at her watch. "Really, I'd just like to get back to bed, and I'm sure you could do with some sleep, too, or it'll be Nancy firing you next time. You know she's just waiting for the chance."

"If you're sure." He leaned forward to kiss her, then back again quickly when she almost shut the door in his face. "Landy?"

"Sorry. It feels weird talking to you at my back door at this time of night. Paranoia's setting in." She raised her face for a kiss that was at best perfunctory. "See you later? Dinner at your house tomorrow?"

"Sure."

Later, after thumping his pillow for at least the tenth time, he hoped she was resting well. At least one of them should be, and it sure as hell wasn't him.

He still felt like an outraged lover.

"Garlic bread. Marble cake—Evelyn Titus's recipe. Cheap wine. And you want to know why I'm kicking your door instead of ringing the bell." Landy glared at

Micah over the top of the cake, but she couldn't make the expression stick. He looked so cute in an apron.

He took the bottle and the foil-wrapped loaf she thrust at him. "We're celebrating," he said, leading the way to the kitchen.

"Oh, yeah? What are we celebrating?" She hoped she wouldn't fall asleep in the middle of whatever it was. Last night, Andie had woken up with a nightmare no sooner than Landy had gone back to bed, some unnamed horror making the child's eyes large and poignantly dark in her small face. Landy had spent the rest of the night in the rocking chair between the little girls' beds while Allie slept in the library. At least, Landy hoped she'd slept—she'd looked no less haunted this morning than she had the night before.

"The *Taft Tribune* was officially making a profit this week. Now, next week, when the light bill comes and we have to pay the monthly advance on mailing costs, we'll be back in the red, but for this moment, we're actually solvent." He beamed at her. "Would you like me to pay for both of us the next time we go out? As long as we stick to high school functions and Burger King, I can swing it."

She laughed. "You dope. Give me a kiss before we eat this garlic bread and before our chaperones show up."

"No chaperones tonight. Pop's over at Nancy's— doing God knows what, I might add—and he told me not to wait up." Still wearing a silly expression, he put the food down and turned to take her in his arms.

Lord, she loved kissing him. She loved the way her

body fit into his, the way his hands stroked up and down her back. When the kiss ended, he looked down into her eyes, his face shaping a smile. And then he kissed her again, deepening it with a teasing tongue.

Anyway, she hoped it was teasing. Even though he never pushed her farther than she wanted to go, she understood that he was bound to become frustrated with her reticence. They were adults, after all, and at least one of them had a healthy libido.

Sure, she liked necking in the kitchen, but she knew that wasn't going to get it done. He wanted a mature relationship, not a pre-adolescent game of Red Rover.

Red rover, red rover, send Landy right over!

Only she wouldn't go. She liked being invited, but she didn't want to play.

"Yikes," he muttered against her mouth. "If the sauce boils over, you're not going to volunteer to clean it up, are you?"

"There are limits," she said, "to what even the most seasoned volunteer will hold up her hand to do. Tomato sauce on stovetops is outside those limits."

He grinned, kissed her lightly again, so that his freshly shaven cheek just whispered against hers, and turned his attention to the sauce.

"Sorry I bothered you last night," he said, when she was setting the table with the pasta dishes he'd bought at an auction held for Colby's benefit.

"It's okay. I appreciate the concern." She couldn't look at him, and for a moment the silence between them was uncomfortable. She looked past him, the silverware forgotten in her hands. "You're boiling over!"

"Oh, sh—Sheba's scissors."

"You're not nearly as good at not swearing as Eli," she said, when she'd stopped laughing.

"I'm not a minister or a father," he said smugly. "I don't have to be, although every time I say so much as 'damn,' Lindsey fixes this look on me that makes me correct it." He moved the sauce to the back of the stove. "Salads are in the fridge. Let's eat."

They strolled the River Walk after dinner.

"It's starting to get dark earlier," said Landy. "It seems as though the kids just got out of school. Summers go a lot faster than when we were younger."

"That's what happens. My dad says his own birthdays don't really surprise him, but mine sure do." He looked at her walkway with consternation as they went past her house. "Want me to drop you off here?" he asked. "I can run your car over tomorrow."

She stopped walking. "Mr. Walker, are you trying to get custody of my marble cake?"

"Yes, ma'am, at least what's left of it after that piece you ate for dessert." He shook his head sorrowfully. "How such a little woman can pack away so much food is—"

She smacked his arm. "You don't want to finish that sentence, do you?" She led the way to her porch.

"Probably not," he agreed, his arm around her waist pulling her to him. "Truth to tell, I'm whipped. Between the watch last night, getting bankrupted in poker and firing Nancy, I'm ready to call it a day." He traced a finger down her jawbone before pushing her hair back from her face. "I'll bet you're tired, too."

"Extremely," she admitted, "and I'll appreciate it if you bring my car over tomorrow." She unlocked the door, stepping inside with his arm still around her.

"Right, and if you need anything before then—" he kissed her once, then again "—you can call me. I'll jump on my white horse and be here in a heartbeat."

"White horse?" she murmured, distracted by his lips. Lord, but she loved his mouth.

"I want to be your hero, and heroes ride white horses."

"Oh." She looped her arms around his neck, raising her face to his once more. "How could I have forgotten?"

It flowed between them, and Landy wondered how there could be so much heat without flame. "Oh," she whispered as his hand slipped beneath the T-shirt she wore and came to rest lightly on her breast. "Oh, Micah."

"Too much?"

She shook her head. *Not enough. Not nearly enough.*

"Then let's—" He reached behind her, releasing the hooks of her silky bra. "One-handed. Wow, I can still do that one-handed."

"Don't make me laugh," she said, laughing anyway. "It makes it too hard to panic."

"Okay." He kissed her again, his tongue searching, not ravaging, the inside of her mouth, and his fingers found her nipple. "Ah."

Her breast swelled into his palm, its tip turning into a tight little bud as he rolled it between his fingers.

When he pulled her shirt free from her shorts and lifted it, she hummed a little sound of protest. Or at least she meant to. It died in her throat as his lips closed over the nipple he wasn't teasing with his fingers.

Oh, she had forgotten how delicious it could be, this touch that was more intimate than a kiss but less so than what came later. She could feel little flickers of delight between her legs and was startled at the yearning they woke within her. She didn't want that, she thought, as his hand moved around to caress the bare skin of her back.

Really, she didn't.

"Whoa." His voice was husky when he raised his head. "I need to go." He reached behind her again, fastening her bra, then put a finger under her chin, lifting her face to his. "I want more. You know that."

"Yes." *So do I.*

It was the first time she'd had the thought. She didn't give voice to it, not yet. But it gave her new hope, that maybe at the end of the long dark tunnel there was some semblance of physical normalcy. She might be able to give and receive love without fear and pain and panic. There was even a chance—

"Give it back or I'm telling Miss Landy you went in her room!" The voice was very young and very loud.

Micah looked up. "Sounds as though you have company," he said quietly, his gaze unsmiling.

"Yes." She wanted to elaborate, but couldn't think of how without betraying Allie. *Don't come into the kitchen, girls, please.* "I—yes."

"Ah, damn it, Landy, just when I think—"

When he stopped, she followed the line of his gaze with her own, not wanting to see what he was seeing.

Not knowing what to say when Allie stepped into the kitchen, in full view from where they stood.

Chapter Twelve

Window on the Sink still on the computer, can't put this in a column because the Tribune *is a family newspaper: Damn. Damn, damn, damn.*

Allison disappeared from sight as quickly as she'd come into view, but Micah had already seen her, and was both offended and angry, though he'd have been hard put to fully explain either reaction. Landy almost ran over him going outside, and he followed her.

"Allison? Allison's your company?" What in the hell was going on here? Landy and Allison didn't know each other beyond nodding if they met on the street. Did they?

"Micah, I really can't go into this now."

And then anger had a reason. Secrets. Dear Jesus,

he was sick of secrets. "Well, when *can* you go into it? When can I stop walking on eggshells, being afraid I'll say the wrong thing, do the wrong thing, kiss you too hard? When are you going to stop keeping secrets in your eyes? Good grief, I *brought* Allison here to Taft. Why on earth should it be a freaking secret that you know her?"

Landy's eyes were dark and sparkling violet. "You think I'm keeping secrets because I never mentioned I knew her? I know Sam at the paint store, too, and Jake at the hardware and Jenny from Down at Jenny's—I know her real well. Of course I know Allison. What does that have to do with whether I trust you or not?"

"Allie works for the paper, Landy. It just makes sense you'd have mentioned it. We talk about Nancy, Joe Carter, even the carriers. You don't think it's odd you never mentioned Allison Scott?"

He knew he was probably saying the wrong thing right now, but he didn't really care. "What does a person have to do to earn your trust, Landy? Go into the ministry? Become a nurse? Because I think Eli and Jessie are the only members of the people-Landy-trusts club, aren't they? Or do you maybe trust Lucas and my father now, too?"

"I have good reasons for not trusting—"

"—me? For not trusting me? What reasons would those be, Ms. Wisdom, because I'm afraid I really don't get it. I'm not your wife-beating husband or his prosecuting father or even one of those reporters you hate so much because they messed up your yard. That was

Allison, your secret company, wasn't it, or does she keep secrets from you, too? Didn't you know she was there?"

Angry accusation replaced the secrets in her eyes. "How did you know that?"

"Know what?"

"That Allison was one of the reporters in the yard."

He frowned in confusion. "We've worked together for over five years, Landy. Why wouldn't I have known that?"

"When you came here, you acted as though you didn't know about Blake and me and how he died. You listened to what Lucas told you and then you let me tell you the whole story again. Why, when you knew all along, did you have to hear it all again and again?"

"I knew about the *case*," he said. "The trial. I knew the 'facts.' I listened when people talked. I never said I didn't already know what they were talking about, never pretended it was all news to me."

How could he make her understand? He'd taken vacation the last week of the trial and sat in the bar a block over from the courthouse to wait for Allison to join him. "How did she look? How's she bearing up?" he would ask when she walked in wearing that particular expression reporters wear when they've been in court, trying to stay awake. And every day he would think but not say, *God, I wish the bastard wasn't dead so I could kill him myself.*

"She's fine. She looks rich." With a barely curious glance in his direction, Allison would order a draft and flip open her laptop. Her stories were terse and accurate, reflecting bleakness and heartbreak. She'd hated the trial. She'd never liked Landy, either, though it hadn't shown in her stories.

Landy's voice brought him back to the present with a jerk. "The case?" Her eyes were wide with hurt and disbelief. "Is that what I am, Micah? A case?"

"No. If you'd been just another case, I'd have covered the story myself. I'd have been waiting in your yard every day and then going over to Clancy's Pub to write my story. But I couldn't separate myself from the girl I knew who walked in the rain for a charity, so I had to hand the regional story of the year off to someone else."

"Too bad," she said bitterly. "You might have been in line for the Pulitzer or something."

"Oh, right, that's certainly what I consider every time I write a story."

"Well, consider this," she said. "Consider us not seeing each other any more. We both want honesty from the other one. You want me to trust you. I'd say neither thing was going to happen any too soon."

And then she was walking away, moving up her path with a stiff dignity that was both awkward and commanding.

He started to call her back, he thought about following her, and he considered leaping into the Twilight to cool off, but before he could do any of those things, she slipped.

She fell nearly to the end of the path before he could reach her, rolling over the uneven brick in a way that was sickeningly reminiscent of the macabre movies that used to run on Fright Night at the theatre. Micah and Eli would flip a coin to decide which one of them had to call his father to pick them up after the movie. Because it was raining, or they were tired, or it was late—anything other than admitting they were scared to walk home.

Oh, but Micah was scared now. That old expression about one's heart being in his throat was dead on. Somewhere deep inside, he was probably still angry, but he couldn't think about that now.

"Landy." Her bad leg lay at an odd angle, one hip higher than the other, and he wanted to make her more comfortable, but was afraid of hurting something. "Landy." Her eyes were closed, but she wasn't— "Landy?" Yes, she was unconscious. *Oh, God.*

"Micah, what happened?" He heard the slam of the back door and looked up to see Allison hurrying toward them, anxiety lining her thin face.

"Call 911. She fell." When she hesitated, he barked, "*Now,* Allison!"

Allison turned and ran back in, and Micah went back to what he was doing. Landy was breathing fine and her pulse was light and fast. If she'd hit her head, he couldn't find evidence of it. *Please.*

"On their way." Allison came down the path carrying a light blanket. "Here." She helped him cover Landy. "What happened? I never heard a thing."

Micah looked from Landy's face to Allison's, stricken by the comment. She hadn't screamed, hadn't even gasped, when she fell. Had abuse made her so resigned she was inured against showing pain?

"There was nothing to hear," he said woodenly. He

looked up at where Allison stood above him on the path, her arms wrapped around herself as if in self-defense, and remembered why she was here. Anger surged again, but he wasn't sure of its source. "Go back inside, Allie, and go upstairs. Protect your children."

"But—"

"Just go." When she turned, he said, "Call Reverend St. John, will you? Tell him to meet us at the hospital."

She nodded and went inside. Micah looked back down at Landy. She was so still, her face ghostly white in the dim light. *Why doesn't she wake up?* He took her pulse again.

As though his fingers, touching warm against the cool skin below her fragile jaw, could keep her safe.

Landy. Oh, God, Landy.

"They can say what they like. It's just like 'simmering rage.'"

"What?" Jessie's voice was close to her ear.

"Pain. It's like...never mind. What are you doing here and why does my leg hurt like this?" Landy forced her eyes open—she absolutely had to slow down on the pain relievers—and looked around. "And while we're on the subject, exactly where is 'here?'"

"You're at the hospital," said Jessie, pushing a button above the bed. "Do you remember what happened?"

Landy frowned, closing her eyes because it was far too difficult to keep them open. "If memory serves, I was fighting with Micah. What time is it?"

"Ten-thirty. Don't worry, you haven't slept through

years of your life. You just got settled in here. I'm sure you were being entirely reasonable, by the way."

"Well, yes, I—" Landy stopped, aware even in her present foggy state that Jessie's and her ideas of reasonable were not in the same ballpark. "It wasn't my fault," she said sulkily.

Her friend's fingers were cool on her wrist. "How did you fall?"

"My leg just folded up on me." Landy moved a little and tried not to groan. She pushed her eyes open again and said ruefully, "It really, truly hurts."

"I know." Jessie squeezed her hand. "Just hang tough, girlfriend. You've been through worse."

"Did Micah come?" She hadn't wanted to ask that, because she didn't want to know. Asking showed interest, and she wasn't interested anymore. She just wasn't.

"Of course. He's in the lounge with Eli, who's trying to convince him it's not his fault you're two parts stubborn and one part a fool."

"Why would he do that? It wasn't my fault," she said again.

"Men always stick together. You know that." Jessie grinned at her. "And then there's the fact that you *are* two parts stubborn and one part a fool, or maybe I've got the mix backwards."

"You're a good friend, Jess."

"I try."

The door opened, and Maria Simcox, who was Landy's doctor and married to the sheriff, came in. She was wearing a sweatshirt that averred it had been stolen from the Sheriff's Department and she was scowling. "I see you decided to wake up, and now I'm missing the end of the movie that's playing in the nurses' lounge."

Landy rolled her eyes, discovering that even that seemed to make her leg hurt. "Everyone's a comedian."

"We learn that in training, when we're only sleeping four hours out of every forty-eight. I think the idea is to cover up for our fatigue-related mistakes by being hilarious. You mean it's not working?"

"The painkillers are what's not working," said Landy. Tears gathered at the corners of her eyes and she sniffed. She felt like a complete baby. "The leg's on fire."

"I know and I'm sorry." Maria's eyes—the flash of which her husband Tom occasionally waxed poetic about and reduced his friends to hysterical giggles—softened with sympathy. "I called Dr. Ramos, who did your previous surgeries. He'll be here soon. You can't put it off any longer, Landy. You're doing further damage with every day you wait. I know this re-injury is hurting like hell, but it may be the best thing in the long run."

"It's risky, though, isn't it? I could still end up losing the leg."

"There's always risk," Maria admitted, "but if you don't have the surgery, you'll keep your leg but you'll eventually lose the use of it to nerve damage and arthritis. No maybes involved—that's a sure thing."

The tears spilled, sliding into Landy's hair before

Jessie could catch them with a tissue. Landy sniffed again and blinked hard, although blinking hurt, too. "This," she said, "has been a hell of a day."

Jessie met her eyes with an unsmiling gaze. "Just remember, my friend," she said again, "you've been through worse."

"So who's the guy who looks like Antonio Banderas?"

Eli straightened so quickly his chair slid back from the table. "Where? Is Melanie Griffith with him?"

"There. He's with Maria."

"S'pose Tom knows?" Eli blinked owlishly at the pair who disappeared into Landy's room.

"Eli."

"Relax, Mike. Antonio is Dr. Ramos, an orthopedic surgeon. He's worked on Landy's leg before, and it's my guess he's going to work on it again."

"Oh, hell." Micah leaned forward, covering his face with his hands. "I'd just finished telling her what a swell guy I was and she fell trying to get away from me. If I was that great, would she have been running away?"

"Yes." The humor was gone from Eli's voice. "She's been running since Blake died, and she can't differentiate between good guys and bad. We're all bad ones and ones who aren't bad yet will be soon." He sighed. "I pray Ramos can fix her leg, but I also pray someone can fix her heart and soul, the crippled parts you can't see."

A few minutes later, Jessie came down the hall toward them. "She's awake," she said without preamble, sitting in the chair Eli pushed out with a foot. "They're in there now, arguing her into agreeing to surgery." She reached for Eli's coffee and drank deeply.

"When can I see her?" asked Micah.

"You can go in when Maria and Dr. Ramos leave. She asked if you were here."

"She did?" Hope flickered, then died. *She was running away.* "She wants to tell me personally to go jump in the Twilight?"

Jessie looked thoughtful. "She didn't mention it, but that could be it." Relenting, she squeezed his arm. "I think she just wants to know you're near, whether she'll admit it or not. If I were a more vigilant best friend, I might resent that."

"As best friends go," said Eli, reaching for her hand, "you're not so bad."

Micah noted Jessie didn't draw away and tucked the knowledge away to tell Landy when he got to see her. If they happened to be speaking to each other at that point, that was. *What's taking so long?*

"Of course," Eli continued, "I don't have much basis for comparison."

"Bite me," said Micah, and got to his feet when the doctors came out of Landy's room. "Maria, can I—"

"Absolutely." Maria jerked a thumb over her shoulder. "Tell her if she goes back to sleep you promise she won't wake up without her leg." She touched his shoulder as he walked past.

He stopped, giving her a bleak look. "Landy's not real big on believing me."

Maria's eyes were solemn. "Show her you mean the things you say." She nodded toward Landy's room. "Go on. My money's on you."

She obviously hadn't seen him play poker.

Landy's room was dimly lit, and she looked ridiculously small in the hospital bed.

"Hey," he said softly, approaching on silent feet. "You still awake?"

"Will you go to my house?" she asked urgently. "Allison and the children are there."

He took her hand. "What do you want me to do?"

"Just be there until arrangements can be made. She's afraid." She smiled drowsily. "Ride your white horse."

"Okay." He kissed her palm and closed her fingers over it. "I'll do that if you'll go to sleep, and I promise you won't wake up without a leg." He chuckled, stroking a finger gently down the side of her face to push her hair back. "Bald, maybe. Maria has a sick sense of humor."

Her answering grin was small, but it was there nonetheless. "Has to have. She's married to Simcox." She closed her eyes. "I'm going to sleep now. You'll go to my house? You'll keep them safe?"

"I promise. And I'll try not to fall off that horse."

"I'm counting on it."

He bent to kiss her. "You do that." Bending over her with his hands on either side of her, he said quietly, "We have to fix things, Landy. If we have any hope for a future, the fact is that I *am* going to fall off the horse sometimes and you're going to have to trust me to get back on without kicking you in the process." He took a deep breath. "And we need to tell each other the truth, even when we're not sure about the outcome."

"I want that, Micah. I do."

He kissed her again. "Then we'll go from there."

Chapter Thirteen

Window Over the Sink, Taft Tribune: *Summer's slipping away quickly. Tans are fading, daytime hours are shortening, and the Twilight seems to lap more quietly at his crooked shores. Aches settle into your bones and your heart and anxiety creeps around corners waiting to attack. You have, out of the blue, far too much time to think about yourself.*

It's a waiting time. For school to start, for leaves to fall, for the first frost.

For the other shoe to fall.

"I'm not going home with you, Jess. You already have your own kids and half the time Eli's to contend with. You don't need a grouchy older one in a cast."

"Don't use the word 'older' so loosely," Jessie scolded. "I'm two months...more mature than you are."

"Yes, but your hair's clean, so it doesn't show."

They shared a grin of understanding, then Landy said sensibly, "I'll just hire someone for a while. I can get around a little bit with the crutches and sleep in the library."

"This is Taft, remember? There's no one to hire since you're out of commission," said Jessie briskly. "Matter of fact, the realty called wondering if you could answer the phone next week from your bed."

Landy quirked a brow. "And you told them?"

"That you'd check your calendar and get back to them."

Landy grinned at her. "Allie and the girls?"

Jessie sighed. "Back home."

A light tap on the door preceded the appearance of Micah's head around its edge. "How's it going? Maria says they're kicking you out because you're grouchy."

"Nah, it's because her hair's dirty." Jessie looked at her watch. "I'm going home. I think Micah has a plan he's going to talk to you about and I don't want to be here for the repercussions." She waved a crumpled bag. "I have your laundry."

"Thanks, Jess. Talk to you later."

Micah crossed the room to kiss her before sitting on

the edge of her bed and handing her the fat-and-calorie-laden vanilla milkshake she'd come to expect every day.

She smiled at him, thinking he needed a haircut but that the shagginess of his dark hair was no detriment to how he made her heart flutter in her chest. The fact that his hair was shiny clean made her even more conscious of her own unwashed state. "Plan?" she said.

"Yup." He looked extraordinarily pleased with himself. "I'm moving in with you."

By the time the coughing stopped, Landy's hip hurt, the itching inside her cast had intensified to the point of bringing her to tears, and she was pretty sure Micah had drawn blood when he pounded on her back to make her stop choking.

"Give me this." He took her shake cup from her and set it on the side table while he wiped her streaming eyes with the stiff tissues that were standard hospital issue. "Are you all right?"

"I think so." She sniffed mightily, blew her nose, and reached for her shake to take a healing draw of the melting ice cream. "What do you mean, you're moving in?"

"Well, shoot, we already go to church together, so we've as good as announced our engagement anyway. My moving in is just an anticlimax."

She met his laughing gaze. "Micah Walker, you are a menace."

"Certainly," he said agreeably. "But, the truth is that you can't stay by yourself for a while. I asked Nancy if she wanted to take time off to be with you, but everyone at the office said if anyone took time off it should be me because my coffee and my disposition aren't as good as hers." He leaned close and spoke confidentially. "If you ask me, they just don't know the real Nancy."

"Don't make me laugh so I choke again!" She shook her cup at him.

"So anyway, I thought I could stay nights and still go to work, regardless of what the newspaper staff thinks. Dad, Eli and Jessie could drop in through the day. Not to mention Nancy on the days I fire her and those seventy-five kids of Jessie and Eli's." He looked smug. "I know Wendy, Hannah and Lindsey would do it if I asked them. Lindsey loves me and Wendy and Hannah think they can soften me up so I won't call them out even if they are."

"Oh, Micah, it's too much to ask of anyone."

"Really?" He gave her a skeptical frown. "You suppose Allison would think it was too much? Or any of the other passengers on the infamous Railroad?"

"That's entirely different," she argued.

"Yes, it is. But one thing's the same." He captured her chin between his thumb and index finger and looked into her eyes. "You're a part of the Railroad not only because of your own history but because you care about those people." His kiss was gentle, sweet and far too short. "I care about you. Okay?"

"Okay." She moved her cup away from his reaching hand. *I care about you.* What delicious words. "But I'm not sharing my shake."

* * *

"Did you sleep well?"

She felt like an aging virgin, lying there with the blankets pulled up to her chin asking him how he'd slept for all the world like he was a normal guest and these were normal circumstances and her hair wasn't still filthy.

He needed to button his shirt.

"Tine. I think Winnie the Pooh is conducive to good sleep, don't you?"

She felt her cheeks burn. "The grown-up quilts are hanging in the closet. You can get them out." *You need to go button your shirt, Micah, and I need to go to the bathroom. And we need to quit having this stupid polite conversation.*

"Winnie the Pooh is fine." He eyed her sharply. "Are you ready for a walk? Like to the bathroom?"

"I'm sure I can get there when the time comes." *If it's not too late by then. Good grief, Grandmother, why did you raise such a prude?*

"No time like the present," he said briskly, crossing the library to where she lay on the folded-out couch. "Come along, Ms. Wisdom. I'll try to get this right, but let me know if I hurt you, okay?"

He moved so quickly and efficiently that she was standing in the bathroom, propped on her crutches, before she had time to protest further. "Where did you get so good at that?" she asked.

"My mother was ill for quite a while. She hated being helped as much as you do, so Pop and I learned to be quick so she didn't have time to think about it." His sigh was deep and almost silent. "I guess we didn't, either."

For a moment, looking at him in the wicker-framed mirror in the minuscule bathroom under the stairs, she saw the angry boy he'd been and knew a moment's sharp regret that she hadn't known him better. And maybe she needed to know him better now, too.

"I'll be upstairs." He pointed at the old-fashioned teacher's bell on the sink. "Ding that real hard if you need me."

She laughed. "Does Nancy know you have that?"

"Sure does. I stole it right off her desk."

By the time she'd done all the bathroom errands required and some of the ones desired, Landy was exhausted. But determined. She *would* walk the fourteen steps from the bathroom to the library by herself.

Or maybe not.

"I hate this," she said on a sobbing breath when Micah found her leaning against the wall. "I'm thirty-six years old, for heaven's sake."

"With a cast on your leg and several incisions that haven't even begun to heal. Give yourself a break, Landy. Even debutantes break bones."

He'd buttoned his shirt.

She tried to laugh, though the attempt sounded sickly. "But they do it with dignity and unadulterated grace."

"Coffee will help," he promised. "I even called Nancy to find out how she made it so it would be close to right instead of the sludge I make."

The couch had been folded back into daytime status, but pillows and a quilt were still there, waiting for when she needed to lie down again. Which her throbbing leg assured her would be soon.

Micah settled her in with her leg up. "Back in a minute. Do you eat breakfast?"

"Not till later. I can fix it."

"I know."

But it was already fixed. The tray he brought had everything she could possibly need, including coffee, a rose in a bud vase and the cordless phone.

"Aren't you going to eat with me?" she asked, then immediately backpedaled. "I'm sorry. You've done enough. I don't mean to sound pathetic." *Even though I am.*

"I will," he said, glancing at the clock. "Give me a minute to get my plate and cup. And stop being so damn polite. I really think we've come to know each other better than that, don't you?" He made for the kitchen.

He was right.

But she'd never shared this house with a man. And there was another part to that story: she didn't think she wanted to. As attracted as she was to Micah Walker and as much as she enjoyed his company, sharing space with him was something else again. He didn't even like fingerprints on television screens, and she wasn't ever going back to a place where little things like fingerprints could escalate into big things like beatings.

"What are you thinking?"

She'd been so absorbed in her own thoughts that she

jumped when he sat in the chair nearest her couch and set his coffee on the table beside hers. Pain whirled, and she sucked in her breath, clamping her teeth on her bottom lip for a moment before she could speak.

"Nothing." Her cheeks burned with the lie. She looked down at her tray, focusing on the oatmeal. How had he known she ate oatmeal? It wasn't something she'd told him. "This looks good."

"It's good for you," he said. "Nancy's doing a series on women's health and she keeps bringing all this stuff in that's specially healthy for women. The guys eat it, too. After all, it's free."

"Thank you for fixing it."

"You're welcome. Nancy taught me how when she told me how to make the coffee—she's still at her best in a classroom situation." He put down his spoon and regarded her, unsmiling. "I know it's hard, not being in absolute control. Believe it or not, it's uncomfortable for me, too, staying here and knowing you hate it, that you still don't trust me. We have so much unfinished business."

She met his eyes, sharing the grim look until the silence seemed to fill the air like a cloud. Finally she said, "You should have told me. About your relationship with Allison. How much you knew about Blake and me."

"And you should have told me, too, that you even *had* a relationship with Allison."

The ringing doorbell interrupted, and Eli followed its sound into the room.

"I'm sorry to do this on the first day of Landy-sitting," said Eli without preamble, moving and talking in full-scale ministerial mode, "but Colby's back in the hospital with a barely signifying blood count. I have to go." He bent to kiss Landy's cheek. "I was looking forward to beating you at Scrabble. I could, you know." Even his voice sounded deeper, and he wore a sweater and Dockers instead of the shorts that were his summer uniform.

"In your dreams." She gave him a hug. "Drive carefully, and take my prayers to Colby and his family."

"Will do."

With a thump on the arm for Micah, Eli was gone. "I wish he'd slow down," she worried. "He drives too fast at the best of times, and this certainly isn't that."

When Micah didn't answer, she looked over at him. His face was tight, his mouth a grim line and his eyes the color of pewter. Even his hair, almost always messy, looked rigidly in place. "Micah?"

"I don't think he's going to make it this time, regardless of all the prayers and everything the doctors can do," he said, his voice so devoid of expression it was almost painful to listen to. "I think God's decided we're going to lose this one."

He got up and went to the window, turning the wand that opened the blinds. It was eight o'clock, but it seemed to be barely daylight and the day promised to be a gray one. Even the Twilight looked listless.

"There's always hope," she argued. "He's come back before when no one thought he would."

"He's a baby, Landy. He weighs twenty pounds on a *good* day. What's he got left to fight with?" He kept his back to her, making it difficult for her to hear him. "He trusts the rest of us to do his fighting for him, and we're failing him. I don't know how, but we are."

"That's what happens when you trust, Micah, and that's why I can't. Colby doesn't understand that—like you said, he's just a baby. But you're a grown-up, and you know that, sooner or later, the person you trust is going to fail you."

He turned from the window. "You're right," he said, and a jarring note of teasing came into his voice. "It's a hard lesson and I'm even older than your ancient thirty-six. It's time I learned it." He came to stack the dishes on the tray, including his nearly untouched ones. "Jessie will be here soon, so I think I should get to work. Is there anything more I can do before I go?"

He leaned across the tray to kiss her, but the gesture was perfunctory and his gaze slipped almost impersonally past hers. "I'll see you this afternoon," he promised, "and we'll play Scrabble." Laughter jangled in his voice, arguing obscenely with the misery in his eyes. "You may have Eli scared, but I can still beat you."

She smiled back at him, wondering if her eyes were as sad as his. "I don't care what you say, quzex isn't a word."

"Well, it should be." He tapped her nose. "If you need anything, call me at work or on the cell phone, okay?"

"Yes, sir. Is Allie doing all right? She's back at work, isn't she?"

He nodded. "She seems okay, but—" he shrugged "—as you know, she's back at home, too, so who knows how long it will last?"

Allison wasn't in the office, nor was the story she'd been assigned in the computer, though her notes lay in a neat stack beside her keyboard.

Her daughters' pictures, in polymer frames, sat on the desk. The little girls were all rosy cheeks and blond hair, and the oldest one was missing a front tooth.

He had the sudden, jolting thought that Colby would die before he ever got the chance to lose his teeth. The notion stayed in his mind, little Colby's face crowding in with the images on Allison's desk. Children should never be harmed. They should never hurt or die. Not from disease and not from—

"Joe?" Frowning, Micah looked across the desks at the advertising manager. "Has Allison called in?"

Joe's face creased with concern. "No, and neither has Nancy. Allie misses a lot, but she always calls and arranges for her stories to be covered, and Nancy just flat never misses."

"Has anybody—"

"No one home at either of their houses. Or if anyone's home, they're not answering the phone," said Joe.

"Did you—"

"An off-duty cop stopped in to place an ad and I asked him to run by." Joe looked embarrassed. "I wrote Allie's story. I knew she'd be running behind. You'll be able to pull it up in your office. I don't write that well, but we're low on time."

"Story of our lives, isn't it?" Micah started for his office, then turned around. "Thanks, Joe."

"No problem."

"Why don't you go ahead and paste that story in? And don't forget your byline."

"Okay."

Before he'd closed his office door, Micah went back out through it. "I'll be back," he said. "Can you hold down the fort? You can reach me on my cell phone if anything comes up."

"Sure. Let me know if I can do anything."

Outside, he stood beside his Blazer, uncertain what to do but knowing he had to do something, go somewhere. He wasn't particularly intuitive—his mother used to refer to him and his father as thick as bricks—but he knew as sure as he was standing there that something was wrong. Out of place. Like on that children's TV show that used to be on in the morning—*What's wrong with this picture?*

In their investigative days, he'd learned to follow Allison's leads because they were always better than his. "I just knew," she'd say when asked. He'd never understood how she "just knew," but she'd seldom been wrong. He wished she was here now, because he was pretty sure he was "just knowing" about her, and he didn't like it.

He looked down Taft's main thoroughfare and felt as though he were in a movie waiting for the bank robbers to run out of the First Farmers Bank with guns blazing.

Since he wasn't sure where he was going, he drove

at a meandering pace that probably maddened the teenager in the red Mustang riding close on his bumper.

There was something wrong, he thought again, but he didn't know what. Didn't know where to go or what to do.

Susan Billings had written about other shoes falling in her column this week, and that was how this felt.

He turned and drove across the bridge, grinning a little when the Mustang gunned it straight down Main Street. Tom Simcox and his little band of deputies didn't take kindly to that.

He should drive by the sheriff's department to see if Tom or a deputy had gone by Allison's. Micah knew she lived in Twilight View, the subdivision they'd always called the Bowery, but he had no idea where her house was in the crowded, pretty little neighborhood with street names like Long Neck and Cool One and One-For-The-Road.

He wondered if Landy felt better with him out of the house. It had been uncomfortable for them both this morning.

Since he was heading for the River Walk anyway, Micah figured he may as well stop by her house. He certainly wasn't doing any good driving around pissing off Mustang drivers and cursing his own inadequacies. Besides, he was pretty sure he could hear a siren in the distance, which didn't lend itself well to the other-shoe scenario.

Joe must not have been listening to the scanner or he would have called Micah on the cell phone to warn him. As it was, other shoes notwithstanding, he was totally unprepared when he turned the Blazer into the River Walk and saw the flashing red lights on one of the vehicles drawn in front of Landy's house.

Chapter Fourteen

Window Over the Sink, Taft Tribune: *Today we went school shopping. I mostly followed along and paid for things, bewildered by my children's choices in jeans, shoes, even underwear; shocked at the prices of everything. No wonder it's said that it takes a village to raise a child—one couple with two incomes just can't afford it, much less a single mother waiting tables Down at Jenny's. Before coming home, we stopped and bought the every-year things: the pens and pencils and the notebooks with pictures of race car drivers and rock singers on the fronts of them.*

"Oh, way cool," said my daughter to the girl next to her, as they examined a steno pad with

someone with spiky hair and a James Dean sneer on its front. "He is so fine, isn't he? Mom, can I have this?"

What on earth did she need a steno pad for?

I remembered, as I stood there tired and cranky in Wal-Mart, pictures of other rock stars and other sports heroes. And my mother would tell me no, I didn't need another notebook. Come on, Susan, let's go home.

The more things change, I've learned, the more they stay the same. But not all of them.

"Sure," I tell my daughter, and I ask her friend, "Do you want one, too?

"I've got all the younger children, and even if they're being very good, which they're not, it's more craziness than you need. Are you sure you're going to be all right? Hannah says she'll be happy to come over if you need her." Jessie sounded frazzled.

"I'm fine. I passed Crutches 101 with flying colors, remember? Micah fed me breakfast—do you know he can cook oatmeal?—and I'm going to sit here and quilt and watch the movies everyone has loaned me." Landy held up her remote control as though Jessie could see it. "Go take care of the kids, Jessie, and let me know if Eli calls with news about Colby. I have to find my way to the back door. Someone's here." She put her hand over the mouthpiece and called, "Just a minute."

"You want me to hold on till you know who it is?"

"No, I'll just stick the phone in my pocket."

By the time she reached the door, droplets of perspiration were rolling down her forehead and her palms were damp where they gripped the crutches. It was enough to make her think longingly of a wheel chair, not that her bungalow had any doorways wide enough to accommodate one. She'd had to hire someone to remove the front door and its frame, complete with sidelights, in order to move her furniture and appliances in when she'd bought the house.

She peered out to see who was on the porch, and her eyes widened when she saw Nancy, holding a child in one arm as she supported a weaving Allison with the other.

"Oh, no."

Sweaty fingers fumbling, Landy turned the locks and jerked the door open. "Nancy, what—"

"I'm sorry, Landy. Allison didn't want to come, but I thought Eli might be here to help and we could move more quickly than usual getting her and the children settled somewhere." Nancy looked back over her shoulder with an urgency that nearly overbalanced both her and her burdens. "I don't know if he knows where we came or not."

"No." Allison's voice was slurred, and when she lifted her head, it was all Landy could do not to gasp. The young woman's cheek was slashed from the corner of her eye to the edge of her mouth, a long, thin cut that had barely broken the skin. "He doesn't know."

Landy stepped aside awkwardly so that they could enter, lifting a hand from her crutch to stroke Britt's hair back from her face when she passed.

The little girl looked up, and Landy bit down hard on her bottom lip. A vivid bruise bloomed below the bright blue eye, an eye that was bloodshot now and looking much older than the almost-six Landy knew its owner to be.

"Oh, baby," she breathed. She raised her eyes to meet Allison's, hoping no accusation showed in her face. "You need to go to the hospital," she said quietly.

Nancy released Allison and reached for Britt's hand. "The library?" she mouthed over the two blond heads.

Forgetting her need to lie down, Landy nodded.

Allison watched her children accompany Nancy from the room before turning back to Landy. "The hospital is the first place he'll check," she said, her voice desperately tired. "I didn't want to come here, but the bruise on Britt's face took away my last option."

She leaned against the counter in the kitchen, even more ashen than when she walked in. The shallow slash stood out like a scarlet beacon on her face. "Nancy stopped to give me a ride to work because my van was broken and walked right through the gates of domestic abuse hell."

In the distance, a siren wailed, and the two women stared at each other. "I didn't call the police," said Allison faintly.

"Sit," Landy urged. "I'll get some—"

Before she could finish, Allison slid bonelessly to the floor, her head thumping sickeningly against the leg of the barstool as she fell.

"Oh, God." Landy stumped to where the other

woman lay, scrounging in her pocket for the phone as she went. She got down—she would never know how—and was examining Allison's head when Nancy came back into the room.

"They're watching *101 Dalmatians*. Thank heaven for Walt Disney." She stopped short before hurrying to where Allison lay on the floor. "What in the world—"

Landy thrust the phone at her. "Call 911."

But there was no need. The whooping sound of the siren had stopped abruptly, followed immediately by the ring of the doorbell and thumping on the front door.

"Landy? Nancy?"

The door opened before Nancy reached it, and Micah and Tom Simcox burst through the opening, looking like a modern-day, testosterone-based version of Keystone Cops.

Micah came to Landy's side. "Are you all right?" he asked. "Did you fall?"

"I'm okay. It's Allie. I think she's fainted."

Tom backed up to the door and waved his arm. "Come on in," he called, "but if you turn that damn siren on again, I'll arrest you just on general principles." He hurried over to where Micah and the women were clustered at the bar. "A new ambulance driver. Came from Louisville to live in the country and hasn't learned yet that by-the-book means something altogether different in small towns where we write our own books. Nancy, did you do this?"

She whacked him one. "Get a cold cloth," she ordered, "and a bag of frozen peas. Micah, get Landy onto her feet before she freezes in that position and they have to operate on the other leg. What are you boys doing here anyway?"

Tom spoke from the depths of the freezer. "When an off-duty deputy went by Ms. Scott's house on the request of Joe down at the paper, no one was home, but he looked through the kitchen window and saw some blood. A neighbor, thinking the deputy was a Peeping Tom, came over and threatened him with a broom, then told him she'd seen Nancy's car take out of there like a bat out of hell. Will corn work?"

"Yes, fine. She's coming around nicely." Nancy turned a piercing look on the ambulance driver and attendant. "Thank you for coming, but as you can see, you're not needed. You may return to the hospital."

"We can't do that, ma'am," said the driver, offering a patronizing smile. "We've been called—"

"You heard the lady." Lucas Trent's voice spoke from just inside the door, that courtroom voice that no one ever ignored. "Ms. Wisdom thought she needed your help when her leg wouldn't cooperate, but obviously she's fine and being helped by friends and family. Is that right, Landis?"

"Yes. Yes. I just panicked, is all." Landy didn't lie very well, so she kept her attention focused on Micah.

"Mr. Trent's right," said Tom. "You all need to get back to the hospital. If you've dealt with my wife before, you know she won't take kindly to not having an ambulance if she needs one."

"Sorry…uh…sorry for the false alarm," Landy stammered, moving her gaze to Allie's pale face.

When the ambulance had gone, its lights off and its siren silent, Lucas said, "I think I'll continue my walk and perhaps tell everyone I meet that Landis had a fall but she's fine. Would that be workable?"

"Very," said Landy from where Micah had arranged her in front of the fireplace with her leg on a hassock. "Thank you, Lucas."

"I'm going to pick up my wife for lunch," said Tom. "She'll want to have it here so she can get a look at your leg, Landy. She'll take care of your face, Ms. Scott."

"Thank you, Sheriff." Allie didn't meet his gaze. "For everything."

He went toward the door, but turned back before opening it. "You can file charges then."

"Charges?" She looked vague. "He didn't mean—"

"Mommy?" Britt's voice preceded her into the room. "Andie and me are hungry."

Landy felt fury rolling not just within her but through the entire room. She looked from the child's marked face to the row of butterfly bandages marching down Allison's face. "You were saying, Allie?"

"You can stay here until you decide what to do." Landy looked across the table at where Allison sat with her laptop computer. "The house isn't a depot for the time being, but another township will move you on if that's what you'd prefer. I can't guarantee your safety. I think it's probably only a matter of time till your husband figures out that you're here, and this is his first arrest—he'll have himself out of jail in a heartbeat."

Landy smiled, hoping the expression was heartening; it had taken real courage for Allison to file assault and battery charges against her abuser. "This lets Micah off the Landy-sitting hook. You're so much help when you're here that he can go back home."

"Micah's staying, too," he said from behind the newspaper. "Somehow I have trouble thinking a woman in a cast and another with stitches in her face can do a lot to protect themselves if someone really wants to do harm."

The women exchanged a look. "Any minute now," said Landy, "he's going to tell us not to worry our pretty little heads about a thing."

Allie smiled for the first time since she'd arrived that morning.

Micah laid down the paper and spoke to Allison. "I don't like losing you at the *Trib,* but I think we both know you're not going to stay. Do you want to go back to Lexington?"

"We need somewhere new, I think, somewhere that the kids can forget and I can start over." She laughed, a dry little sound. "I was going to say, 'Somewhere safe,' but that's an illusion, isn't it?"

"Take your time," Landy suggested. "School doesn't start for several weeks yet, so you have some time to make your choice and find a place to live."

Allison sighed. "Time's another illusion. I have to earn money to support my family, and I can't do it by lingering over alternatives."

Landy and Micah began in unison, "I can—" but Allie shook her head.

"No." She came to hug Landy, a move both unprecedented and unexpected. "Back when you were on trial, I helped you into the house one time when you stumbled, but in the end, you were on your own, getting through the hard parts by yourself." She stepped back and straightened her narrow shoulders. "It's time for me to do the same thing."

It was past midnight when Micah followed shadowy light and uneven footsteps into the kitchen. "Can't sleep?" he asked.

"I keep waking up," said Landy. "I thought I'd sit on the porch and watch the river, but I seem to be having trouble negotiating the crutches and the door at the same time."

"I can probably help with that." Micah opened the door, the clicks of the locks sounding loud and foreign against the natural sounds of the night. Then he took the crutches from her and swung her into his arms. "I won't drop you," he promised, "or at least no further than the bottom of the steps. Can you push the door shut? My hands are sort of full."

"What kind of hero are you?" she asked, her laughter falling soft against the side of his neck. "Expecting me to close my own doors. Next thing you know, you'll want me to pick up the tab at McDonald's."

"What can I say?" He sat down carefully on the half of the swing he'd come to think of as his own, keeping her tight in his arms and making sure her cast-covered leg rested on top of his. "Inflation's at an all-time high."

He pressed her cheek to his shoulder. "Comfortable?"

She nodded, her hair brushing against his chin. "Isn't the river beautiful tonight? Makes you wonder how the day could have been so awful when the Twilight just trolls along as though nothing had happened."

"I think a river's like a Psalm. It provides comfort whether you realize it's going to or not. I'm not a very good Bible reader, but the book opens right up to Psalms. They even give you the words to prayers if your mind won't find them on its own."

Micah was horrified that he'd revealed this part of himself to anyone, much less the woman in his arms who couldn't bring herself to trust him at the best of times. He didn't think waxing religious on her back porch was one of those.

"I think of Britt and Andie and wonder how much of this they'll remember," she mused. "Is there some kind of built-in protective device that will allow them to put it all behind them?"

He rubbed his hand down her arm when he felt the gooseflesh rise on her skin and wondered if she was asking the question about herself as much as the children inside.

"Hey," he said, "we never got to neck today. That can't be right, can it?" Her lips were so close, her eyes shimmering velvet-like in the dusky light filtering up from the River Walk.

He lowered his mouth to hers, feeling her lips soften and open under his. He kissed her until they were both breathless, their hearts jumping around like the frogs he could hear down by the river.

It was amazing to Landy how quickly the unlikely residents of her home created a routine. In the space of time required for her to go from crutches to a walking cast, they became a family unit, albeit a strange one.

"I feel like a dad." Micah spoke through the screen door one night after carrying a dozing Andie up to bed. He went back to the refrigerator for some iced tea and stepped onto the porch.

"With Eli and Jessie's kids, I'm the guy they can con into an extra story or an ice cream when the truck goes by. Even with Colby, I'm just someone who cares from a distance. But with these two, I have to tell them not to run through the house, not to talk back to you and their mother. I have to crawl around under the bed and dig out the monsters—I can't just tell them they don't exist."

"It's different," Landy agreed. She nodded toward where Allison sat, waif-thin and alone, on a park bench beside the river. "Jessie and I were always close as sisters—still are—but that one's like a younger sibling. Allie and I will probably never be close in the way Jess and I are, but I doubt we'll ever again be separate, either."

When he sat in the swing beside her, his thigh warm against hers, she rested a hand on his leg, leaving it palm-up so that he could wrap her fingers easily with his. This was what they did, how they sat, where they were in this relationship that was and then wasn't. They kissed if they didn't have an audience for the moment, did some necking if there was a free fifteen minutes, and proceeded to gasping and yearning if no one was home at all.

"What are we, do you think?" he asked, taking her hand. "The girls are the children, Allie the troubled younger sister. We're not the parents, since they already have parents, so who are we in this family we've gathered?"

"Well," she said lightly, "one of us is a case of arrested adolescence who just can't seem to deny a hormonal attraction to whoever you are. However, I can't gather the nerve to go through with what those hormones are screaming for." She smiled at him, moved her face just a little so that she could kiss him, then withdrew just as slightly. "And who are you, Mr. Walker?"

"Why, I'm the baddest of the badasses, Ms. Wisdom. Brewery trash who found his way across the river." His arm slipped behind her to draw her even closer. "Come to lead you astray." His lips came down to hers as his hand slid inside her blouse, his fingers finding her aroused nipple without fumbling at all.

"Oh." Her voice was airy, catching in her throat and coming out on a sigh. "Lead on, anywhere you please."

His eyes and hands went still in the space of a heartbeat. "Anywhere?"

Their shared gaze was full of questions asked and answers given. Hopes and wishes and maybe-this-times floated in the air between them. Landy, who hadn't danced in at least fifteen years, felt as though she'd surely be light as a feather on her feet, walking cast, aching hip, and all, if only Micah would ask. If only he would lead.

The sound of footsteps on the path drew them apart, and they turned as Allison approached.

"What's on your mind?" asked Micah.

She sat in the chair that faced the swing. "I've had a job offer," she said. "In Cairo, Illinois, of all places, for a newspaper, the *Citizen*. It would be like the *Trib* in that I'd be doing a little bit of everything but could still pick my kids up from school and pursue the writing of the great American novel."

"Hmm," said Micah, looking up at the porch ceiling.

"And today there was another offer in New York, features editor for a magazine called *The Woman's Way*. It's published by a woman named Dee St. John-Ellery."

Micah's feet, which had been on the porch rail, hit the floor with a bang. "That's Eli's ex-wife."

She nodded. "It's more money, more chance of professional growth." Her smile was a mere tug at the corners of her mouth. "A bigger expense account, so no more beers in saloons across from courthouses."

"But?" Landy moved restlessly, the ache in her hip becoming a steady throb.

"But it's a high-powered job. I not only wouldn't be picking the kids up at school, I wouldn't be tucking them into bed all the time, either. While I'd have an opportunity to help women who have been in the circumstances I'm in, I'm not sure it would be the best thing for the kids."

Allison's face was bleak. "To tell the truth, I'm not

sure I'm the best thing for them, either. What kind of mother waits until her child's injured before she leaves the situation that caused the injury?" She looked at Landy, her expression accusatory. "You wouldn't have. You wouldn't have kept going back even when you knew your children were at risk."

"We don't know what I'd have done because I didn't have children," said Landy briskly.

Micah's arm tightened around her, and his breath whispered across the top of her head when he spoke. "So what do you think, Allie?" he asked.

"I don't know," she admitted. She offered another smile, even slighter than the last had been. "I think I'll go on up. Is there anything I can do for you first, Landy?"

"No, thanks. Sleep tight."

The screen door closed behind Allison with a quiet click, and Micah said quietly, "You wouldn't have, you know."

"Wouldn't have what?"

"If you'd had children, you wouldn't have stayed with Blake at risk to them."

It was a question she'd never really asked herself, but experience with the Railroad and other areas of her life had shown her that people didn't always put their children's needs first. Blake's mother had left when he was prepubescent and been available only spasmodically the rest of his life. Eli's ex-wife had given up custody of her children—all of whom she loved dearly—rather than change her life to accommodate them. Even Jessie, the most devoted mother Landy knew, had arranged her children's lives around her husband's surgery schedule.

"We were raised by our grandmothers," Landy remembered telling her, "and it worked out great, but we never got to be loud or dirty or messy or any of those other things. Why are you doing this to your kids?"

"It works, Landy. We all love each other and it works." Jessie had been polite, but the words "butt out" had been between the lines.

And it *had* worked, but Jessie's children were considerably noisier than they had been when their father was alive, as well as dirtier, messier and occasionally badly behaved. Though they missed their father, in some ways they were happier, too.

Landy relaxed in Micah's arms when he reached down to rub her hip. "Once the cast is off, and you won't have to compensate for anything anymore," he said, repeating Dr. Ramos's words almost verbatim, "your hip will stop hurting."

"I hope so." Which she did, because the steady throb drove her crazy. But she really hoped the cessation of pain didn't mean Micah would stop rubbing her hip.

Chapter Fifteen

Window Over the Sink, Taft Tribune: *The wind was blowing so hard yesterday, it whipped the hems right out of my sheets. There was a coolness in the breeze that hadn't been there just the day before.*

"Winds of change," said my neighbor, as he helped me take my fraying bedding from the clothesline, "blow cold and hard."

"Are you sure this is what you want to do?"

Allison looked up from the box of personal items she'd just removed from her desk. "No, not really," she admitted. "But Illinois's not far enough—he'd find me there in a heartbeat. New York offers anonymity, and the Railroad will help with an identity change if I decide we need that."

Micah jerked his head at her, and she followed him into his office. "I'm sorry," she said. "I know I've been more trouble than any employee's worth."

"You're not just an employee," he said. "It's like Landy said, you're the little sister who was born when we were old enough to be resentful but still young enough to be proud."

"Thank you," she said.

"For what? Being Landy's and my little sister probably isn't that cool."

"For your friend in Cairo. Even though it didn't work out, it was kind."

Micah thought briefly of Jill and of her husband who'd never tried to break the connection that remained between his wife and her ex-boyfriend. Ben was a big bruiser of a guy who probably could have crushed Micah rather handily if he'd ever wanted to. "Why would I want to?" Ben had asked. "You're the loser, not me."

The loser looked at Allison, thought of Landy and Jessie, and was grateful that at least one of the women in his life had indeed found a winner.

"And for being my friend," Allison continued. "Even when we were sitting in bars together while we were reporting, you kept yourself separate, but coming back to this little town has made you more than a boss, more than a saloon buddy when we're on a story. If anyone had told me then that you'd end up knowing about my personal life in any context except running a series on battered women, I'd have said they were crazy."

She came to where he stood behind his desk and put her arms around him. "I'm glad to be wrong about that."

He held her for a moment, gingerly because of the birdlike fragility of her. "Be safe, Allie." He released her and took an envelope out of his top drawer. "It's cash. I didn't want any check-cashing records if your husband hires someone to come looking for you." He raised a hand, using his thumb to rub at the tears on her cheek. "Keep in touch when you can. Kiss the girls for us and remember there's always a home here for you and for them."

She went still, her eyes dark and heartbreaking in their pain. "You know if anything happens to me, they're yours and Landy's. Mr. Trent has all the papers."

"We know." He kissed her cheek, warm where his thumb had stroked it. "Be safe," he said again.

He watched through the glass half-wall of his office as she hugged Joe and shook hands with the others in the newsroom until she came to where Nancy waited.

The retired teacher folded the slight reporter close, and when they separated both were in tears and Allison held another envelope.

A wasted hour later, Micah left his office with little more than a wave to the others and drove straight to the bungalow on River Walk. He started to open the door, then remembered he'd moved back home a few days before, when Landy had gotten her walking cast. He knocked.

"It's done," he said when Landy limped to the door. "She'll be all right now, so why do I feel so rotten?"

He looked down at the embroidery hoop she carried. A quilt block was stretched across it, and when he lifted his gaze to her face, he saw what the morning's fare-wells had cost her. Besides an adopted little sister she didn't always like, she'd said goodbye to two children whose every sticky kiss had been treasured and tucked away in her heart for safekeeping.

"I love you," he said.

She didn't know who was more surprised: Micah when he said it or herself when she heard it. She stood in startled silence, the quilt block in its hoop hanging from fingers that had suddenly lost all feeling.

"Would you like to have lunch?" she asked.

"Yes."

"Come in."

She pushed the door wide so that he had room to come in, then forgot to close it until he reached to place his hand on hers on the knob.

And then she said, "I love you, too."

"So where do we go from here? You're the debu-tante. You know these things."

She lifted her arms to encircle his neck, the embroi-dery hoop dropping unnoticed to the floor. "You're the reporter. Maybe you should investigate."

"Like research?"

The kiss was so long and leisurely, she almost lost the thread of the conversation, bringing herself back to earth with difficulty when she felt her blouse slipping down her arms. "Uh-huh."

"Sure. Where do you want to start?"

Her bra joined the embroidery hoop and her blouse on the floor, and he dipped his head to draw one tight little nipple into his mouth.

She stopped breathing for a space, concentrating on the buttons of his shirt. She had two of them undone when one of his hands delved inside the waistband of her shorts.

She gasped for air. "How about my room?" The shorts slid over her hips and she stepped out of them blindly. They slipped easily over her cast and over her other foot—hadn't she been wearing a shoe?

"I sort of had it in mind to end there."

Landy wasn't sure how they got to the closed door of her bedroom, but it seemed to take quite a while. Somewhere in the back of her mind was the knowledge that she was with a man, naked except for her white cotton panties and a walking cast. The scars she had always tried to hide weren't covered at all.

She hesitated, eyeing the closed door.

"It's up to you," he said, his voice soft and Sam-Elliot-velvet. "Believe me when I say there's no nobility there—I'd damn near rather die than stop, and if we do, I'm going to spend the next week inside that lacy curtain in your shower with the water on cold—but I'd rather that than hurt you."

The passion was like a live thing between them, in their stroking hands and the energy of their lips and tongues meeting and colliding. Landy wanted to weep with the need that clawed at her insides.

But even as she reached for the glass doorknob, she felt the scream begin to build. It started as a flutter behind the desire, and pushed the need out of its way until it pulsated at the back of her throat, ready to escape at any moment.

"Oh," she said. "Oh, damn. Damn you, Blake Trent. Damn you."

Her tears poured over Micah's fingers as his hands cupped her face, and she closed her eyes rather than see the disappointment and the dying passion in his. "I'm sorry," she said. "I'm so sorry."

"Don't cry." The Sam Elliott voice was little more than a whisper. "But don't let him win, either, Landy."

She looked up, blinking against the tears that continued to trickle from her eyes. "Win?"

"If remembering Blake controls you even now, when he's been dead all this time, he's winning. If he can convince you from the grave that I'm going to hurt you, he's winning. If we don't go into that room…"

"He's winning," she finished. "And he is. When this cast comes off, even if I don't limp anymore and I can run down steps and dance and bend my knee, I'll still be crippled. I thought maybe I wouldn't, you know." She raised her eyes to meet his waiting gaze. "I thought when I stopped hiding the scars on the outside, the ones on the inside would just go away. But they're never going to, Micah. Never."

"Never's a long time," he said, leaning against the wall and pulling her against him so that some of her weight shifted from her casted leg.

"Don't you see?" she said. "I've been living a pretend life. Pretending that just because I wanted you, I could have you. I did the same thing with Britt and Andie. Each day was another day I could pretend they weren't going away. Did I ever tell you they'd slip sometimes and call me Mommy, just because we were together so much? And after a while, I stopped correcting them because the pretense was so sweet."

"Landy." He reached to take her hand, but she pulled it away.

"I was doing the same thing with you," she said. "It felt so good. I thought, how could something this wonderful go wrong? But of course it could."

"Landy," he said again. "Do you remember that before we came upstairs I said I loved you?"

"Yes." Oh, how sweet it had been hearing those words and saying them back. Why hadn't she just hugged them to her and not asked for more?

"Do you know that I still do?"

"You can't." But even as she spoke, she became once more aware that she was nearly naked in the arms of a man who'd said he loved her before the bedroom door even opened. And said it again after she'd given in to fear one more time.

Blake's winning.

"No," she said aloud, "he's not."

Inside the room, in Micah's arms, she hoped for magic and there was magic. In his kisses and the touches of his hands and his mouth on her flawed body. It was almost as though he celebrated her scars—"They make you who you are"—and he caressed them, every one.

"They won't go away," she whispered again, but he silenced her with his mouth on hers. And when the scream tried to find its way into her throat, he silenced it, too. With yet another kiss, a gaze that smiled into her eyes, he stilled a sound she hadn't even made.

"I want who you are," he said softly, "and if the scars go away, part of you does, too." He laughed, the sound vibrating against the sensitive skin behind her ear. "Can't have that happen."

He moved over her, being careful of her leg, and joined their bodies slowly, soothing her fearful jerks with long strokes of his hands.

Against all odds, she hoped for completion and she achieved it, reaching gasping, joyous release in a way she never had before, "Oh," she said, "oh, dear God."

She wasn't sure breathing normally again was a likely option, but eventually both her mind and her body quieted. "Thank you," she said in a wispy voice that didn't sound like her own.

There was a smile in his voice. "No thanks necessary." He moved, keeping them joined, so that his weight didn't crush her.

She looked up, meeting his eyes. "Show me what to do for you."

"Do what you want," he said. "Do what feels right."

"This?" She was tentative, feeling like a virgin in her naiveté. "Or this?"

"Oh, yeah." Sam Elliott's voice again, gentle and

wild at the same time, against her throat, as he brought her to a second orgasm along with his own.

She hoped for trust, for inner scars to be instantly healed over by the power of love, for fear and silent screams to be forgotten parts of her past. She hoped to be able to give him all of herself, holding nothing in reserve to keep her safe later. She hoped to fall asleep in his arms and rest dreamless and warm and full of hope.

But trust slipped away as quickly as her clothes had, and she grew restless almost immediately, trying to draw the blankets over herself without being obvious about it.

Micah leaned up on one elbow and looked down into her face for a long moment. "I should go back to work," he said, and dipped his head to kiss her. "Don't get up."

He moved so quickly, getting up and carrying his clothes into the bathroom, that she felt bereft. "Micah?"

A few minutes later, fully dressed and with his hair semi-neat, he came back to the bed. "It wasn't enough, was it?"

She could hear his disappointment and knew her reticence was the cause of it. "It was wonderful," she said. "*You* were wonderful. But when you've been scared for a long time, it's hard to let go of it all at once."

They kissed goodbye, whispered disjointed words of love, and he left. He'd been right; it wasn't enough, but maybe next time. Maybe then.

"We want to get married, and we'd like to have your blessing."

Micah stared at his father and Nancy, dumbfounded.

They were all standing on the polished floor of the living room in the St. John house. The windows were open, and Micah could hear the river lapping against its shores.

Married? He felt as though he'd fallen into the middle of an old musical, one of those with two song-and-dance men as protagonists. One of those stars had just gotten the girl, but two days after making love, Micah and the partner of his dreams were still dancing around the gazebo, avoiding each other's eyes.

Ethan looked younger than he had since the day Micah's mother had been diagnosed with ovarian cancer. Always a handsome man, he was even more so with happiness radiating from his eyes and his arm around a nice woman.

"You do realize," said Micah, "that if you fire her, she doesn't leave. That if you think you have the last word, you don't. That if you want something really fattening and filled with cholesterol, she brings you a bowl of oatmeal." He turned his attention to Nancy. "And you do realize that he snores. That he hasn't hit a hamper one time in the thirty-eight years I've known him. That if you take him you have to take me, too."

Nancy and Ethan smiled at each other, then at him, and he stepped forward to create a three-way hug. "For what it's worth," he said, "you have my blessing." He kissed her forehead, then his father's cheek, before stepping back. "Do you have anything else to tell me?"

Ethan frowned. "Like what?"

"You don't, like, *have* to get married, do you?"

After further discussion of dates and logistics, Micah headed toward the door that led to the River Walk. "You two probably think you're entitled to some privacy now, so I'm going for a walk."

"This isn't your night." Micah flicked a glance at Eli when the minister joined him a few minutes later. He didn't want company, especially good-natured company who would offer to pray for him.

"Yours, either."

"I'm not on watch. I'm just walking. Alone."

"Me, too. Or I was walking alone. Now I'm not."

Micah bit back a curse. "I'm not very good company."

"So? What else is new?"

They walked on in the comfortable silence of old friendship for nearly a half-lap. "It was good of your ex-wife," said Micah, "to help Allison."

"Dee's part of the Railroad," said Eli. "There's a much larger network there than here."

Micah nodded. He should have figured that one out on his own, but he hadn't. "Nancy and Pop are getting married."

"Ah." Eli stopped, bending to pick up a few pebbles. He sent one skimming over the water's surface. "Three skips. Is that all right with you?"

"Yeah, it's great to see them so happy." Micah tossed a pebble. "Duh. Two."

"It gives me some hope," said Eli, and there was a note of wistfulness in his voice Micah hadn't heard before. "About second chances. Sinker."

"Landy needs some of that hope," Micah muttered. "Three."

"So give it to her. Two."

"What do you mean, give it to her? Sinker."

Eli threw his last pebble and stood in thoughtful silence for a moment under the dim golden glow of the pseudo-gaslight. "Forgive me if I'm overstepping here, but do you know the old saying 'yes, but will you respect me in the morning?'"

"Yeah."

"Well, truth be told, Blake Trent probably loved Landy as much as he was able, pitiful though that was. But he never respected her. He used and abused, and left her there to hate him and herself, with no hope at all."

In unison, because they were thirty-eight instead of eighteen and they were tired from skipping stones and trying to understand women, they sat down. "What makes you so sure of this?" asked Micah.

Eli hooted. "Sure? I'm not sure at all. This is still Taft, Indiana, where men better not be caught talking about their feelings and a woman better not discuss hers with any man she hasn't been married to for at least twenty years or sleeping with for half the football season. I'm just judging by what little I've heard Landy say and the even less I've been able to pry out of Jessie."

Micah leaned forward on the bench, staring out at the quiet water with the gold light dancing on its surface. "I think you may have a point, Pastor."

"Well, don't let it get around. Something else about Taft, Indiana, is that Methodist ministers aren't allowed to know about sex. Even Methodist ministers with six children. It's not enough not to practice it, we can't know about it, either. I'm pretty sure it's a city ordinance."

Chapter Sixteen

Window Over the Sink, Taft Tribune: *I love fall, with its vibrant colors and crisp sounds, but it makes me so sad! Because no matter how I look at it, no matter how long I try to make my days by rising before the sun and going to bed late, autumn is about endings. Flowers wilt, grass browns, trees become barren and stark. Even the Twilight slows its meandering ways until sometimes I look at it and wonder if it, too, is dying.*

And so I sit here wrapped in fleece and doldrums. And mourn summer's passing.

"Well, of course you're going to have a church wedding. Catch this thing, Landy. Your leg's in a cast, not your arms." Jessie flipped a tablecloth over one of the long tables in the church basement in preparation for the Autumn Blood Drive.

Nancy came from behind the counter carrying two small, square bowls full of sugar and artificial sweetener packets. "I'm sixty-one years old and gravity has not been my friend over the years. I really can't see me in a white dress and veil now, can you?"

Landy exchanged a grin with Jessie. "We weren't really suggesting the whole white dress and veil thing, but we do think your old students would welcome the chance to throw things at you, even if it's only handfuls of grass seed tied up in little circles of tulle."

The older woman's exaggerated sigh nearly blew the cloth off the table, sugar containers and all. "You girls are so mean to me. Do you think it would be all right? Just a small wedding with a reception here in the basement. People wouldn't think it odd, an old bat like me going down the aisle like a sweet young thing?"

"What do you care what people think?" asked Micah from the doorway. "And where are Maria and the nurses who volunteered for this? I came early because my receptionist didn't show up so I have to man the phone at work." He scowled at Nancy. "You're fired."

He folded his future stepmother into a hug, and Landy made her way to her work table, thinking she could do with a hug herself. "Do you have your Red Cross card?" she asked when he approached, pushing the clipboard with the sign-up sheet toward him.

He laid it on the table. "Cast come off tomorrow?"

She nodded, "I have to go into Louisville to Dr. Ramos's office, though. Do you want this donation on Colby's list?"

"Yes, please. I'll take you to Louisville, if it's all right, and—" he raised his voice "—if I can get Nancy to come to work so I can be out of the office."

"Keep a respectful tongue in your head, young man, and I'll consider it," she called from the kitchen. "Have you eaten this morning, Micah, or will you faint when you're halfway through the blood-sucking process?"

"He's had his breakfast." Maria Simcox, high heels clattering, came into the room. "He and Tom and Eli were together Down at Jenny's creating all kinds of trouble. Jenny asked me to come pick Tom up before she had to call the deputies on him."

She went to the kitchen to wash her hands. "Blood-sucking probably isn't a real good term to use today, though. We have enough trouble getting guys to give up a pint. They think all their testosterone's in it."

"You ready, Micah?" Jessie smiled as she laid a solicitous hand on his arm. "Maria always draws the first pint, and she loves getting a good start on the testosterone collection."

"Fine, fine. If I walk out of here talking in a high voice, you ladies will be sorry. That's all I've got to say." With a long-suffering sigh, Micah followed Jessie to a blood-drawing station, pressing Landy's shoulder as he passed.

His thumb raised with the gesture, stroking gently

along her jaw line. The affection in the touch was palpable, and she smiled extra-wide as she greeted the next donor.

"A wedding! Those girls are talking about a real wedding! And Nancy's going right along." Ethan leaned back in his chair Down at Jenny's, looking disgruntled. "Good Lord, we're in our sixties. What do we want with a wedding? People will give us toasters, for heaven's sake, and we've already got two households worth of stuff."

"I double-dog dare you to march right over to the newspaper office and tell her you two aren't kids anymore." Lucas smirked. "Be sure and mention the part about you both being in your sixties and too old for a wedding."

"All we need in this town is you old geezers going off inciting a damn riot," muttered Tom Simcox, pouring sugar into his coffee. "Nothing like a lawyer to go screwing things up for the rest of us. Landy getting that cast off today, Micah?"

"Yeah." Micah looked at his watch. "I'm taking her to Louisville." He grinned at Ethan. "After she gets done at the doctor, I'm sure she wants to go shopping for wedding stuff. Do you want some spats to wear over your nice shiny patent leather shoes?"

His father favored him with a scowl. "I'll tell Lindsey you're off to the big city with another woman."

"No problem. I'll bring her back a big candy bar she doesn't have to share with the rest of the menagerie and all will be forgiven," said Micah, getting to his feet. "You buying my breakfast?"

"Only if you promise you won't even look at spats."

Micah stopped at the florist's on the way to Landy's, and when he arrived at her house and she opened the door, he presented a mixed bouquet of multicolored chrysanthemums. "For luck," he said, and drew her into his arms for a long and satisfying kiss. "For me." He kissed her again, and when they were both somewhat breathless, he said, "For more luck," and kissed her once more. Finally, he gently pushed her away. "Any more luck and we'll be in real trouble. You ready for the big un-casting?"

"More than ready," she said, taking silk roses from the vase on the credenza inside the door and replacing them with the mums, "even though it does mean shaving this leg again. Wendy and Hannah told me the braided look wasn't in this year."

She arranged the bouquet as she talked, and Micah leaned against the door frame to watch her. He thought of his father and Nancy, with their laughter and teasing and their unabashed love for each other and wondered if he and Landy would ever share that.

Well, perhaps he was making progress; it used to be he wondered if he could ever feel "that way" about anyone. Now he knew he not only could, but he did and probably had for a long time. And would, for much longer.

"I'll be just a minute," she said as he left the door and approached. "We've got plenty of time."

He remembered words from one of the children's books in the nursery at church. He'd held Colby in his lap and read it aloud just last Sunday, bringing the rest of the toddlers to attentive silence at his feet. Colby's fuzzy new hair had tickled his chin, and he'd had trouble forcing the words past the lump that grew in his throat.

As he continued to read the book with a hoarse voice, he'd thought of Britt and Andie and how much Landy loved and missed them. He realized he felt the same way—about the little girls and the red-haired boy in his lap. His voice had failed altogether, and Lindsey had had to recite the rest of the story from memory.

Did anybody really have plenty of time?

He took one of the flowers from her hand, stroking its soft petals down her even softer cheek. "'I'll love you forever,'" he quoted, "'I'll like you for always.'"

Landy slept on the return trip, leaning back against the pillow Micah had tossed into the backseat before they left. With the cumbersome cast removed, she'd been able to feel the full effect of the repair that had been done to her hip. The resultant euphoria and several disbelieving trips up and down the corridor of Dr. Ramos' office suite had exhausted her.

She woke when the Blazer stopped in Micah's driveway, and sat up straight, rubbing her eyes. "Merciful heavens," she said. "I slept all the way home."

"The Lord loves a quiet woman who doesn't backseat drive," he said solemnly. "And it's all right if she snores."

"Is that right?"

"Well, it's what my father always said, so if I'm wrong it's his fault. Sit still. I'll come around."

When he opened her door, she asked, "What did your mother say when your father acted out that little performance you just did? You know, about the backseat driving and the snoring and all."

"My mother was a lady," he said. "She smacked him a good one."

"I thought so." She leaned just far enough into him to kiss him. "Like that?"

"Not sure." His hands urged her closer to the edge of her seat, closer to him. "You better try again."

"What do you think?" he asked a few minutes later, his lips hovering over hers. "Wanna go steady?"

"You're just asking that because I got my leg fixed and I have this fancy new scar."

He patted her hip. "Not to mention all that sexy dark hair where your cast was. I can hardly stop myself from jumping your bones whenever I even think of that."

She looked past him at the front entry of what was still known in Taft as the St. John house. "What are we doing at your house?"

"Having dinner. You mind? You should be well-rested and all."

"You cooking?"

"We'll see." He lifted her out of the Blazer, setting her down carefully to avoid jarring her. "Ready?"

"Uh-huh."

Music was playing quietly when Micah pushed the door open. "Your dad must be home," Landy murmured. "Good. I can ask him about that backseat driving thing." She stopped to listen. "Peewee King?"

"'Tennessee Waltz' was the only waltz I knew." Micah closed the door and turned back to her. "Hey, debutante," he said, slipping an arm around her waist, "can I have this dance?"

She had thought, really, that she would eventually get over loving Micah Walker. They'd stay friends, of course, and when he found someone who could do all the things wives and lovers did, he'd marry that woman. Landy would go to their wedding and take a lovely gift that matched the house she'd helped decorate. Maybe a set of towels with cunningly entwined monograms. She'd keep her back broomstick straight just the way Evelyn Titus had taught her, at least until after the reception was over. Then she'd come home to the lonely bungalow down the Walk from the St. John house, pop the cork on a bottle of grocery-store wine and drink herself into a stupor.

She could do that. She'd shot the first man she loved and lived to tell the story, for God's sake. Marrying off the second one would be a piece of cake.

At least that's what she thought before she waltzed with him on the waxed hardwood floors of the St. John house. Through the foyer and the library and the living room with a fire already burning in the fireplace. They did a fancy little twirl around the dining room table, slowing their steps when their feet found the carpet of the family room.

By then, she knew she'd love him forever.

Chapter Seventeen

Window Over the Sink, Taft Tribune: *Every year,
I think the holiday season's excitement will
escape me, leave me untouched by its glitter and
noise and joy. But it never does. I am caught up
every time in the belief that the world is at heart
a good place and that peace on earth is more
than an impossible dream.*

"We'd all love for you to come, but are you sure it's
safe?" Landy spoke quietly into the phone, as though
a whisper would fool anyone who was listening.

Allison's sigh rattled like the purr of a cat against her
ear. "No, but I can't raise these kids to be afraid, either.
Nancy and Ethan have been wonderful to us. I don't

want Britt and Andie to miss their wedding. This will be a chance for them to have Thanksgiving with their grandmother and to see the Christmas lights around the River Walk. We can stay through Tuesday so all the decorations will be up."

"I'd love it. I miss you all."

"We miss you, too." Sadness crept into Allie's voice. "The kids miss everything in Taft, and they don't really like it here yet. This move was good for me, but I'm not sure it was the right thing for them."

Landy opened her mouth to answer, then closed it again. It wasn't up to her to tell someone else how to raise their children.

"We'll be there Wednesday night. Dee's flying in to see her children—the magazine owns a jet—and the girls and I are coming with her. A few days out of school is no problem."

"I'll be waiting."

She felt cold after hanging up, even though her pea coat was still half-on from where she'd run to answer the phone when she and Micah had come in from a morning walk.

"They're coming?" Micah pulled off the coat, then drew her into his arms when she shivered. "What's wrong?"

"It just scares me. I know her husband's lying low since he got out of jail, but he's out there somewhere. I'm afraid she's walking right back into the fire and taking Britt and Andie with her. But I didn't know how to say, no, don't come."

* * *

"You know, I don't remember this part." Eli put away the last dinner plate with an exaggerated sigh. "When we were talking about a traditional Thanksgiving dinner, no one mentioned that we'd be doing dishes while they made little things of grass seed. It's not like grass is going to grow in November anyway. They should throw birdseed."

"Yeah, and some litigious individual would sue the church because the seed rolled under his shoe and made him fall down," said Nancy around the ribbon between her teeth. "Lucas would run out of the church just to take names."

Landy got up and went to look toward the Twilight. She could see Lucas on the park bench across the river, staring into the water. "He seems so lonely," she said, and looked toward Ethan. "Did you invite him today, or did you think I wouldn't want him to be here?"

"We weren't sure," said Micah. "You and he have come a long way, but we thought maybe spending holidays together was pushing it a bit."

"I asked him. He wouldn't come," said Ethan. "Holidays are extra painful for him, I think."

Although Landy and Lucas had "come a long way," the steps had been small ones. A ride home from another Railroad meeting, tea in a thermos when he was on watch, waves across the Twilight when they were both outside. Lucas had not given blood the last time, and he seldom attended church although he continued to donate generously to its coffers. He had stopped emblazoning "in loving memory of Blake Trent" on the memo line of his checks, though.

Landy turned from the window. "I think I'll take a walk. I'll be right back."

Winter was a frosty promise in the air around the river. Even though the afternoon sunshine tried to convince you it was warm outside, it wasn't. Landy walked fast, reveling in the freedom of her repaired hip.

"Do you remember that first year Blake and I were married?" she asked without preamble when she reached the man sitting on the park bench. "I left the giblets in the turkey and the butter out of the mashed potatoes and the gravy never got thick—it poured out like colored water. And you just ate. 'Good flavor,' you kept saying. And then you helped with dishes while Blake watched football and, over tea that you made, you told me what my parents were like. Grandmother never wanted to talk about them, but you let me see them as they must have been, and it gave me permission to mourn. Did I ever thank you for that?"

She sat down beside Lucas, tucking her hand through his arm. "That first night you rode home from the Railroad meeting with me, when we talked in my kitchen, you gave me that again. I was able to grieve for Blake in a context other than how sorry I was to have been the one to cause his death." She didn't look at him; the words were hard enough to say without chancing seeing accusation in his eyes. "It's Thanksgiving Day. You're the closest thing to a father I ever had. I'd like to spend the rest of it with you. We're getting ready to have dessert over at Micah's, and I promise I didn't make it."

For a minute after her long speech, Lucas didn't speak, just kept his silent, brooding gaze on the Twilight. She was afraid she'd gone too far, pushing him once more into the cocoon of hatred and loss that had defined their relationship after Blake's death.

She watched the river, too, as its waves winked silver and gold in the sunlight, tossing fallen leaves into the air with every movement.

"It did have good flavor," he said. "And I'd like some dessert." He smiled, the expression uncannily like his son's had been. "I hope Ethan didn't make it, either. I'd trust him with my life, but food is something else again."

She laughed. "No, but watch out if he offers to make the coffee. Micah came by his lack of skill honestly."

He got to his feet, pulling her with him because her arm was still in his. "Why do you think we drink beer on poker night?"

They walked slowly toward Micah's house. "I know the surgery took care of your limp," said Lucas. "Did it fix the pain, too?"

"Most of it. It still lets me know when it's going to rain."

"It's a funny thing about pain," he said. "You get used to it. It becomes a part of you, so much a part that sometimes you don't even notice when it's gone. Like when you're walking under an umbrella and all of a sudden you look up and the sun's out. You feel so foolish."

"But if you look around," she said quietly, "you'll see someone else walking in the sunlight under an umbrella. Feeling foolish isn't an unusual or private thing."

"Are you trying to tell me I'm not special?"

"You're asking that of a woman who fell down her own sidewalk?"

They laughed together, the sound an almost eerie echo of bygone days. "It's time," said Lucas, "for both of us to go forward, isn't it, Landy?" He looked away, his mind and heart going to a place she couldn't follow. "It's time to bury Blake."

"Getting married the Saturday after Thanksgiving is fine," Micah grumbled, plugging in his Christmas tree and eyeing the sparkling lights. "Having a wedding and reception is fine. The rehearsal dinner was great tonight. But a honeymoon? In November? What am I supposed to do for a receptionist when everybody calls in scores for the high school basketball pool next Friday? I need Nancy."

He straightened with a groan and stood back to look at the Douglas fir in front of the windows that faced the river. How had the three-foot Christmas tree he'd consented to buy become an eight-footer with a thousand twinkling white lights on it?

"Calm yourself, Mr. Editor. I'll come in and answer the phone," said Landy, filling his coffee cup. "Did you ever decide what to give them for a present?"

"Uh-huh," he said, and cast around for a new subject. "I'm going to build up the fire. It's colder than a witch's parts out there."

"Well?" She sat down, flinching a little. He wondered if her still-touchy hip warned her it was probably going to snow.

He peered out the windows toward the river. "The wind's blowing, too. We didn't have any blizzard warnings, did we? It'd be a shame if the wedding had to be postponed because of weather."

"Micah?"

"What?" He sat beside her on the loveseat and drew her close to his side. She felt so good there, as though she belonged. He hoped it felt the same way to her.

"What did you decide on?"

He sighed. "Tickets."

"Tickets? For the November honeymoon, I assume?"

"Yes. Nancy was on the Internet every blessed minute at work, looking for cheap tickets to damn near anywhere. She wasn't getting any work done, so when I asked her where they'd really like to go and she said St. Croix, I just bought the tickets to get her to go back to work before I had to fire her."

"Plane tickets are nice. If I'd known, I would have chipped in toward their hotel room instead of doing the gift certificate thing."

He felt the heat rising in his cheeks and released her, leaning closer to the fire so he'd have something to blame his red face on. "Nah, it's a honeymoon package. Everything's included."

She smiled at him. "You're a good son, Micah Walker."

"Where would you choose for a honeymoon?" he asked.

"I don't know." She shrugged, and he felt tension in the movement. "You?"

He was silent for a long moment, his thumb stroking absently along the delicate line of her jaw. "Here, I think," he said quietly, tipping her face so he could kiss her. "Because it doesn't get any better than this."

Her own society wedding and the years that followed had given Landy a jaundiced view of weddings in general. Oh, she'd gone to them. She'd blown bubbles, thrown grass seed, and served innumerable glasses of punch and pieces of cake. She'd bought enough monogrammed towels to set up bathrooms for a dozen large families.

She'd stopped buying the towels years before, though, when she got to thinking how few of the marriages lasted long enough to wear them out. "What do you do with them after a divorce?" she asked Jessie the last time she'd bought them. She looked critically at the large S with the smaller *R* and *C* twining through it. "I mean, this is good as long as Rob and Cindy are married, but what if happily ever after ends after six months?"

Jessie grinned. "Car wash rags, Landy. Everyone needs them."

Which explained why Rob and Cindy Shultz's towels were presented in a shiny galvanized pail with a bow around its handle. Several years married and parents twice over, they still told people that although they'd received numerous towel sets at their wedding, they'd only received one bucket. It had sure come in handy, they always added, for washing their car.

Landy never cried at weddings, never danced at receptions even when the music was slow enough to accommodate her hip, and never stood with the single women waiting for the bouquet even if the bride begged her to.

But then Ethan Walker married Nancy Burnside.

The church was full to bursting. It looked as though every person who'd ever learned either geometry or good manners from Nancy had come to witness her marriage. The daily occupants of the Big Loud Liars' Table Down at Jenny's filled an entire pew, retirees of the Taft school system and former employees of the brewery another three.

"I didn't know there were this many Methodists in Taft," said Eli, all innocence. "Would last week's ushers pass those collection plates again? I think we missed a few."

"If that's the case, we'll be having the reception at St. Charles," said Father Fitzpatrick from the fourth pew on the right.

With a stern look over her glasses and a definite twinkle behind them, the organist (Mrs. Burnside's class of seventy-nine), began to play.

Nancy, radiant in candlelight-colored satin, came up the aisle on Lucas's arm. She handed her bouquet to her matron of honor, another retired teacher, and turned to Ethan.

The marriage service was traditional, with a few add-ons.

"I've loved before," said Ethan, slipping a wide gold band onto Nancy's finger. "Long and well, and I love her still. It is this love, and the raising of this son here, that make me the man I am. I offer you myself and my son, from this day forward, as long as you and I shall live."

Nancy smiled into his eyes. "I, too, have loved before, and I love him still. It is this love, and my love for all these children who have passed through my classroom, that make me the woman I am. I offer you only myself, and their sympathy, for as long as we both shall live."

Soft laughter wafted through the congregation, punctuated by sniffles. Landy met Micah's eyes and smiled at him even as she felt tears trickling down her cheeks.

"It is with pleasure, as well as by the authority vested in me by the state of Indiana, that I pronounce you husband and wife," said Eli. "Kiss your bride, Ethan."

Ethan did, at length, after which Micah elbowed him aside and followed suit with a gentle kiss on both Nancy's cheeks. Then Eli stepped forward and kissed her, too, and shook hands with Ethan before stepping back. "Ladies and gentlemen," he said, "I am privileged to present to you Mr. and Mrs. Ethan Micah Walker."

Applause rang through the sanctuary when the Walkers turned to face the congregation.

Eli raised his voice. "Contrary to Father Fitz's hopes,

the reception is at Micah's house on the River Walk and everyone's invited. If you happen to pass St. Charles on the way and want to drop a coin in the donations box, the Methodists won't object."

The party lasted long after the bride and groom, ensconced in the backseat of a limousine, departed for the airport on a noisy wave of well-wishers and more than a few firecrackers.

"These are illegal," muttered Tom Simcox, and lit a whole string of them. "Need to get rid of them before kids get hold of them."

"Oh, of course." Eli handed him another book of matches. "Keep lighting them. If there's any damage, we'll just blame the Catholics."

"It's easy to tell," drawled Father Fitzpatrick, "that Mrs. Burnside—make that Mrs. Walker—has left the party. She'd have your head on a platter for such heresy, Reverend." He reached for a string of firecrackers. "Whereas, since Micah is now her stepson and she has to be nice to him, we can just blame him."

"Where did they get the idea Nancy has to be nice to me?" said Micah, coming to stand behind Landy on the rear deck of the house. He wrapped his arms around her, and she relaxed in his hold. "Wanna dance?"

"Sure." She turned into him. "Is there any music?"

"You bet." They danced into the relative privacy of the deck's far corner. He kissed her, a leisurely meeting of lips and minds. "There. Don't you hear it?"

She raised her face to his. "Yes," she said. "Yes, I hear it."

Chapter Eighteen

Window Over the Sink, Taft Tribune: *I woke this morning and listened for the voice of God. It has been a nice week, you see, and I thought this would be a good time to hear it.*

"Stay awhile." Micah's gaze held hers, and Landy heard the music again. No, that wasn't right; she *felt* the music. In the soles of her feet and in her stomach and in the warm place between her thighs.

She laughed, though the sound caught in her throat. "I *have* stayed awhile. I'm the last one here. I have houseguests who went home hours ago and probably think they've been deserted."

"Allie knows where you are if she needs you. The

kids were tired and so was she. She's probably welcoming the quiet time."

"I'm wearing pantyhose," Landy said, looking down at her stockinged feet. There was a hole in the hose; her big toe, complete with Siren Call nail polish, was sticking out. "I want to take them off, put on a ratty robe and eat ice cream out of the carton. I'm tired, too."

"You can take them off here," he said, and the smile in his voice sounded like more music. "I'll help you. And I'll loan you a robe. I'll even run bath water for you like the sensitive guys in the movies do, and I'll stay out of the bathroom while you're in there unless you'd rather I stayed and washed your back." He came to her, stunningly handsome in most of his tux. He'd left the jacket and tie lying in the dining room after the arm wrestling tournament that the Big Loud Liars insisted was a requirement for all Taft wedding receptions.

"You looked very nice today," she said, unsteady fingers fumbling with the studs in the front of his shirt.

"You, too." He drew her to him with an arm around her waist. "Want to dance some more now that there are no priests or Realtors or Lindseys around to cut in? The music's still playing."

It took her a moment to realize he meant the music that came from the CD player. It had been playing all evening. She nodded, giving him her hand.

"I love you," he said. "Do you believe that?"

"Yes." She relaxed in his hold, reveling in the warmth of his hands, the touch of his lips against her neck. "And I love you."

He kissed her, and she supposed she knew their feet had stopped moving, but it certainly didn't matter to her. What mattered was his mouth on hers and his hands on her hips holding her firm against—against what she wanted. And needed. And longed and lusted for.

"Please," she said.

"Yes," he said.

"What if—"

"We'll cross that bridge when we get there, or ford that stream, or—"

"I knew purple prose would work, given the proper context," she murmured.

"What?"

She smiled against his mouth and felt his lips lift in response. "Nothing."

Oh, she loved this part, the portion of sex that had more to do with love than with the act itself. The teasing and touching and laughing that was neither violent nor cruel. At the soul of her, where she heard the music, she wanted to sink into the tenderness of it.

But even after Micah and she had made love all those weeks ago, and she'd experienced his gentle nature in the most intimate way possible, Landy still couldn't erase the memory of a much darker past. She remembered kisses that became hurtful in their intensity and hands that bruised tender flesh. She remembered loving words that turned to angry insults about her body, her prowess and her inability to respond.

Maybe during the act she was so afraid of, she could make her mind go to that other place, the one that had kept her sane during the years of her marriage to Blake. She could close her eyes and force an artificial inner tranquility that allowed her to survive the external turbulence of sex. Blake had known, and he had hated her for it, but it had worked. At least, sometimes it had.

Micah held her away from him and looked down at her, his gaze searching. She knew she wouldn't look right, wouldn't say the right things, wouldn't do what he wanted—they'd tried that already, and it hadn't been so successful. Her heartbeat accelerated with anxiety, and she glanced away, not wanting him to see whatever was in her eyes.

The banister was wrapped in garlands of fir and red velvet ribbons with small brass bells tied into the bows. The decorations, which had taken several of them the better part of the night before Thanksgiving to put up, had survived the reception intact except for a place near the top that had pulled loose.

"Let me just fix that," she said, starting up the stairs.

"No." He caught her hand, and they stood like that for a minute, with their arms stretched over the distance between them and their eyes fixed on each other.

She looked away. She needed to find that place, that safe place. "But it—"

"No."

He came up to stand a step below her, keeping her hand in his. "There is the door," he said, pointing down the stairs. "You have a key. You can come and go at will. You never have to stay if you don't want to. These stairs go down as easily as they go up, so if you don't want to finish what we've started, we can just walk back down."

"How many times are you going to try?" she asked. "When are you going to decide, the hell with this, and walk away? You deserve more than half a person, Micah Walker, and that seems to be about all I am."

He smiled at her, though uncertainty lurked at the edges of the expression. "I guess I'll try until you realize you're wrong. You're a whole person, and you're the one I want." His hands cupped her face so that she could no longer avoid his gaze. He kissed her, long and slow and leisurely. And they walked up the stairs.

It had never been like this. Even last time, it hadn't been like this. She hadn't really understood that sometimes the act of love went beyond satisfaction and relief. That there was no room in bed for selfishness. That sometimes it was just fun.

When her touch would have been tentative, he tickled her until she shrieked and giggled and tickled him back. When he kissed a lazy path between her breasts and down her belly to where her softest parts hungered for more, she tried to turn over, to stop the most intimate of caresses, but he held her on her back with gentle hands and Sam Elliott murmurings against her skin. "No, no…" she began but never finished, and her next word was his name, spoken from so far down inside herself she wouldn't have recognized her own voice.

"Oh, my," she said a few minutes later, the word no more than a whispered exhalation.

"Oh, yeah," he answered, chuckling deep.

She opened her mouth to say more, but couldn't.

"You all right?" he asked, moving up her sensitized skin until they faced each other.

"Um…" she murmured. She felt as though she were levitating, her body not touching the bed. Or she did, until he reached down and touched her where the nerves still pulsated with the strength of her climax. She gasped, jerking away. "Ow…" But then he was kissing her again and she was lost once more in the pleasure and the joy.

"You ever heard the words 'tit for tat?'" And she showed him what those words meant, her touch both aggressive and tender as she took him to the same place he'd taken her, a place fraught with joy and wildness and completion.

So now she knew. She lay in the warm curve of Micah's arms and rejoiced. "Wow, the earth really does move." She looked into his face, visible in the light that shone from the open bathroom door. "Thank you."

He stroked her cheek. "Me, too."

"It was never—"

"No. For me, either."

"Really?"

"Really. I've never felt like this before." He laughed, the sound soft and deep in the semi-darkness. "I was thinking a while back that you made me feel seventeen again and I didn't like it much." He kissed her, all warm velvet and soft silk. "I've changed my mind."

"Well," she murmured drowsily, "if you're seventeen, I'm fifteen and out way past my curfew. I need to go home." You didn't leave your houseguests on their own in Taft, Indiana. That was even worse than wearing white shoes before Easter and after Labor Day.

"I know." He moved to get out of bed. "I'll walk you."

"You don't have to," she protested.

"Yeah, I do. You want Nancy and my dad coming back off their honeymoon just to kick my ass?" He stepped into a pair of sweatpants, then stopped to watch her climb from his bed. He looked deliciously lustful.

She grinned, though she could feel the heat rising in her cheeks. "I wasn't going to call and tell them," she said, reaching for her clothing.

He came to her with the red bra that had landed on the floor. "I owe you a bath," he remembered, "and a back wash." He slipped the straps over her shoulders and fastened the hook between her breasts, bending his head to kiss the sensitive flesh before covering it. "Or you could have it now." His hands clasped her hips to pull her to him. "Or in a little while."

The next morning over breakfast, Landy was subjected to twenty questions by her young guests.

"You caught Mrs. Nancy's flowers. That means you'll be the next one to get married," said Britt, touching the red roses in Nancy's throwaway bouquet. The bride had tossed it into Landy's arms with a changeup pitch that had the high school baseball coach talking springtime draft. "Does that mean the next one just here in Taft or anywhere in the world, because you'll need to start planning your wedding soon if it's in the whole world. Can I be a bridesmaid?"

"Well, we'll see," said Landy weakly, wondering just how much a first grader knew about catching bouquets.

"I want to be a flower girl. Are you going to marry Mr. Mike?" Andie pushed her cereal around in its bowl. "I don't like oatmeal."

"You did yesterday," said Allison, exasperation threading through her voice.

"But I don't today," said Andie reasonably.

Landy gave Allison a troubled look. Yesterday at the wedding reception, the younger woman had been light-hearted and hopeful. Today she seemed more like the bruised victim she'd been weeks before.

Andie sighed so heavily that it seemed to shake her small body. "Lindsey said oatmeal is really porridge and that's what the bears ate in that story and I don't want to eat what bears eat. Bears are hairy and smell bad."

"Goldilocks ate it, too, and she was beautiful and smelled like wildflowers. Her hair was blond just like yours," said Landy, glad to have gotten past the bouquet discussion with no further questions.

"Daddy says blondes are dumb," said Britt, twisting the end of her curly corn-silk-colored ponytail around her finger. "And they don't mind their own business, he says."

Landy caught the small fingers and began to unsnarl the ponytail. "Sometimes even daddies are mistaken."

Allison had stopped halfway between the bar where

the children sat and the sink, Andie's still-full bowl of oatmeal in her hand. "When did Daddy say that, Britt?"

The words were calm, Allie's expression mildly inquiring, but her eyes looked like a thunderstorm, and her knuckles went first red then white where they gripped the melamine cereal bowl.

"Last night," said Britt. "He called while you were in the shower." Tears flooded her eyes. "I'm sorry. He told me I mustn't tell or we'd all be in trouble again."

She began to cry in earnest. Andie, her still-babyish features a study of confusion, followed suit.

"Why did you answer the phone?" Panic and anger skittered through Allie's voice, the loud sound making gooseflesh on Landy's arms. "You know you're never supposed to answer any phone before the answering machine comes on."

"I know," Britt said, flinching away from her mother's fury, "but Andie doesn't remember it all the time. When I took the phone away from her, I heard Daddy's voice and I couldn't stop listening. I couldn't, Mommy."

"Of course you couldn't." Landy lifted the sobbing little girl into her arms. "It's all right, sweetheart. It'll be okay." She shook her head at Allie.

There was something wrong when a child was taught to screen telephone calls before she had even learned to read, when she was terrified of her father but still wanted to hear his voice.

Landy remembered the early months after she and Blake were divorced. She didn't take his calls for a long time, until the fear subsided, but she used to listen to his voice on the machine. Over and over and over, until a thought began to worm its way into her mind. *Maybe this time.* Then she stopped listening. She'd stopped hoping at the same time, because she finally knew better.

But Britt and Andie were six and five; they shouldn't have to stop listening to a voice they loved; they shouldn't have to give up hope.

"You know what?" Landy kissed Britt's wet cheek. "I went out and rented all the Christmas movies I could think of because I knew you were coming. How do you two feel about wedding cake and milk for breakfast while you watch *Santa Claus is Coming to Town* in the library?"

"Sometimes I still spill my milk," Andie confessed, wiping her nose on the sleeve of her flannel pajamas.

"Sometimes I do, too," Landy confided, shooing the children ahead of her toward the room where the television was. "It doesn't hurt a thing."

Ten minutes later, the two women faced each other across the expanse of the counter and cups of steaming coffee. They'd called the sheriff, though there was nothing he could do except keep his eyes open. "We'll have to go back to New York," said Allison.

But now it was Thanksgiving weekend—Santa Claus was coming into town tonight and the River Walk would become a fairyland of Christmas lights. How did one go about explaining to flaxen-haired little girls who'd already lost too much of their innocence that he would find them eventually if they had to go home early? That no matter how much they loved this little town where everyone called them by name, there was more safety in anonymity?

"I thought you were going to stay till Tuesday," said Landy. "Maybe for now you could spend a few days with your mother in Lexington."

"What?" Allison stared at her. "We're all in danger now. You are, too. How can we stay until Christmas?"

"Don't you remember what you told me, that you couldn't raise those children to be afraid of everything?"

"It was easy to say when he didn't know for sure where we were."

"I know it was." Landy thought of Micah, and tried to recapture the joy she'd felt with him, the sense of wholeness she'd thought she'd never know again. Suddenly, it eluded her just as it had all these lonely years.

"I'm afraid, too," she said, flat and toneless. "I'm always afraid. Of everything." She met Allie's gaze across the counter. "I don't want that for them. Do you?"

"No, but I want to keep them safe."

"I do, too, but I also want them to see the Christmas lights around the river and to think their toes are going to freeze right off when we go caroling."

Landy didn't even pretend to be emotionally aloof from Allie and the girls. It was almost a mantra with the Safe Harbor Railroad, *Don't get personally involved with your guests.* It was something she'd steeled herself to during her time as a host. She sniffled over children after they'd left, as she changed the bedspreads and sewed their quilt blocks, but then she dried her tears and let them go.

It was only when she stitched black headbands onto the quilt block hats that she was unable to let them go. Sobs replaced sniffles, and undiminished anger replaced the feeling of hope she always had for departing guests.

But in any event, the Scotts weren't her guests anymore. In some important if indefinable way, they had become part of her family.

The bungalow felt far too quiet after Allison and the children left for Lexington the next morning. Landy ran the vacuum cleaner over the potato chip crumbs on the library carpet, dug Barbie clothes out from behind the couch cushions, and spritzed the television screen with Windex to remove the fingerprints.

She remembered an earlier conversation with Micah and reached for the phone in her pocket to punch in a number. "Micah? Would you like to come over for dinner tonight?"

"Can I stay for breakfast?"

It would be different this time. He would not sleep on one of the twin beds in the guest room or on the sofa in the library as he had after Landy's surgery. He would share her frilly, rose-strewn bed, tossing lacy pillows onto the floor and pulling the top sheet completely free from the mattress in an effort to get comfortable.

"Do you snore?" she asked.

"Probably. Do you?"

"Maybe a little. Just deep, ladylike breathing. Can you deal with that?"

"I think so."

She didn't even have to take a deep breath, didn't have to chase shadowy memories from the dustier corners of her mind. She could hear the joy shimmering through her own voice when she said, "Then I think you should stay."

The day reminded her of the months-ago first date with Micah, all anticipation and dread. She washed her hair, manicured and pedicured her nails, did a bikini wax and decided maybe it was a good thing she didn't wear bikinis anymore. The preparation was far too painful.

"For heaven's sake," said Jessie, pouring coffee for both of them and staring in consternation at Landy, whose gaze was locked on the window of the oven door, "You've been seeing each other for quite some time now. Why is tonight so important that you're obsessing over a pot roast?"

Landy sipped absent-mindedly from the cup Jessie pushed toward her. "It's just different somehow. So are you, by the way," she added. "You're cranky. You don't sound the least bit like someone whose children are spending a few days with their paternal grandparents."

"I know." Jessie sighed, the sound so deep it sounded like something tearing inside her, and shrugged. "Most of the time, I'm too busy to be lonesome. Then when the kids are gone, nothing is enough to fill up the loneliness—it's just all-pervasive."

But she'd had Jessie.

The telephone rang. After a mad search, she found it in the drawer where she kept dish towels and answered breathlessly on the fourth ring.

"Hey, Debutante, how do you *really* feel about rain checks?"

Landy wasn't sure how Micah managed to sound both excited and apologetic, but he did. "Depends on how you feel about warmed-over pot roast," she said, giving a regretful thought to the wasted bikini wax.

"I'm fond of it, I promise. Hang on," he said, his voice fading on the last word.

He was back in a few seconds. "The president's stopping off in Louisville tonight and doing a sort of casual this-is-the-kind-of-guy-I-really-am thing, drinking coffee with reporters and giving off-the-cuff interviews on the state of the union and how he and the missus are spending Christmas. I just got a call inviting me to come. You're a lot cuter than he is, but I'd really like to do this interview."

"Okay," she said, "just this once, especially since you said I was cuter than a man who's overweight and losing his hair."

"Hey, why don't you come with me? We could stay in Louisville and still have breakfast together."

"That would be fun. I'll—" Her gaze fell on Jessie, standing at the windows that faced the Twilight.

"Not this time," she said, hoping he could feel her regret even though she kept it out of her voice. "Jess is here. I think I'll give her your share of the roast."

"Oh."

"And the wine. I'm going to have that bottle Nancy gave me the night of her shower."

"Oh, I see." She could hear the grin in his voice.

"But we'll think of you while we're eating and drinking," she assured him. "Every minute. At least till Jessie gets drunk, then God knows what she'll do."

"Is this like a guilt-trip thing?" he asked.

"Well, maybe," she said thoughtfully. "Is it working or should I collapse in tears?"

"No. I can't see you from here, so it would be wasted, although it might be good practice for the theatre group if they ever decide to do passion plays."

"Might be." She knew she was smiling, knew Jessie was watching her with *"aha"* written all over her face, but was powerless to stop grinning. It blossomed from inside out.

"I need to go." She could feature him squinting at his watch, then reaching for his glasses so he could see it. "I'm staying over there tonight. See you tomorrow?"

"Okay, providing you don't come up with any more presidents to use as excuses for avoiding me."

"I'll work on that."

She and Jessie did serious damage to the pot roast and then sat before the fire, telling secrets, sharing heartaches and laughing as the wine bottle emptied.

It was after eleven when Eli stopped by on a solitary stroll around the River Walk.

"Coffee?" said Landy. "Are you on watch tonight?"

"Uh-huh." Eli accepted the cup she passed to him

and sat beside Jessie on the loveseat. "It's been pretty quiet, just a few broken windows over at Twilight View and some damage to Down at Jenny's front door a few nights ago, general holiday stuff, Tom says."

"So," said Jessie waspishly, "did your ex-wife get back okay?"

Ah. Landy almost grinned. There it was. The real secret. The heaviest heartache. The alonest part of Jessie's loneliness.

"Why don't you walk her home, Eli? She's getting so crabby."

He frowned at Landy, ignoring Jessie's outraged glare. "I don't know. What if she bites?"

"What if she does? You've had your shots." Landy made a shooing motion. "Go on, both of you. I'm sleepy. It's been a long several days and we're only halfway through the holidays."

She was already in bed when the phone rang from the table beside her.

"I wanted to tell you I loved you before I went to bed," said Micah's warm voice. "It seemed only right, after I chose a balding middle-aged man over you."

She leaned on one elbow, holding the phone close to her ear and grinning with the pure delight of the conversation. "I love you, too."

"What are you doing right now?"

"Falling asleep, now that you've told me you loved me even more than the president, or at least that's how I'm taking it. Did you see him?"

"Sure did, and I was right. You're a lot cuter."

"Thank you."

"You're welcome. You save me any of that wine?"

"Not a drop. Jessie was depressed."

He chuckled. "Eli has been, too."

"He walked her home," she said drowsily.

"I'm going to hang up before you fall asleep. House all locked up?"

"Um-hmm."

"Goodnight, Ms. Wisdom. Sleep tight."

"'Night, Mr. Walker. You, too."

Chapter Nineteen

Window Over the Sink, Taft Tribune: *My grandmother, the wisest of women, used to say, "Better
the devil you know than the devil you don't."
Events in my life and the lives of my friends have
clouded my thoughts on this issue. Although I've
never been a fan of using "Times change" as an
excuse for things, I must admit that things in my
grandmother's time didn't prepare us for some of
the devils today.*

Including those we know.

The noise was at once familiar and unknown.
Someone was in the house.
She'd locked the doors on her way to unplug the

living room Christmas tree. But locked doors wouldn't keep out anyone who really wanted in, would they?

Where was the gun? It was somewhere here in her bedroom, somewhere it could be found and used if it was needed. She knew it was. Blake had always insisted on that, hadn't he? He used to get so mad at her for keeping it in the safe that she'd moved it. Then she'd used it and Blake was dead. She'd gotten another to replace it when she couldn't bear holding the old one again, but where was it?

Lying in her bed, frozen in fear, Landy didn't even glance at the clock, but the sky she could see through her bedroom window had the opening-up look it gets before dawn.

Yet it was so dark. Hadn't the Christmas tree in front of the bedroom window been lit when she fell asleep? Hadn't the moon been large and bright? Or did the moon just disappear once the morning sky began to break? She couldn't remember.

The stillness of her room was peculiar. Normally the heat tapped in its aluminum ducts as it made its way upstairs and the grandfather clock in the hallway ticked loud and pealed even louder. But she couldn't hear anything tonight; neither the heat ducts nor the clock. Not even the groans and creaks all old houses make.

And then she heard a sound, and when she turned toward it, she heard her own terrible and trembling gasp as a blade traced lightly across her throat. There wasn't pain, but she smelled blood immediately.

And then there was pain. So much pain.

It was happening again. She'd been too happy. She should have known such joy wasn't meant for her. Oh, God, she should have known. In the days she'd thought were finally behind her, Landy used to close her eyes and take herself away from what was happening, praying all the while that it was only a dream. It never was, of course, but sometimes, if there wasn't too much pain, she could almost convince herself.

Almost.

And this time, there was too much pain.

"Where are they?" The intruder's voice was soft, almost gentle. "I don't want to hurt you. I don't want to hurt anyone. But you need to tell me where they are."

"Who?" she whispered, although she knew. She knew.

"Britt and Andie. Where's the bitch taken them?"

"I don't…you're hurting me…why are you doing that? I don't know where they are."

The blade slipped across her neck and pierced the delicate skin below her ear, and she had the hysterical thought that if she lived through this, she could probably wear a little hoop earring there. Micah would be entranced with it, she was sure.

Oh, Micah.

"I can wait for you to tell me," the voice went on. "I can be very patient. But my knife isn't patient at all. Did you see what it did to Allison's face? Such a pretty face, and the blade just sliced it right open—I keep it nice and sharp."

He breathed a sibilant sigh, warm against her skin, that made her gag. "So much blood," he whispered.

Is that what felt so warm? Was it Landy's blood, dripping from all the places the knife blade punctured?

The thought made her head swim; she couldn't even watch when the nurses drew her blood at the Red Cross.

"Don't act like you're passing out. Hellfire, you killed your husband, so don't try to convince me a little blood bothers you." His quiet chuckle was too close to her ear. "Of course, this being your own might make a little difference."

He pushed the blade again and Landy cried out. She remembered where the gun was, but she was losing her strength too quickly to even attempt to reach it.

"Should have minded your own business, bitch. All I wanted was my family and for Allie to be a good wife. There was no need for you to get involved, but you just couldn't stay out of it, could you?"

The knife moved again, and Landy closed her eyes on a sobbing breath. She tried to lift her hands to fight him, but her strength, pitiful as it was, was gone, and her hands felt too heavy. The life she'd wanted to live, fought to live, was over before it started. *Oh, Micah, I'm so sorry.*

He couldn't believe he was driving all the way home from Louisville near 4:00 on a winter morning when it wasn't necessary—he could have spent the night in a hotel. The traffic had been light once he'd gotten away from the city, but he was tired, and he cranked up the CD player, playing the Beatles loud and long until he pulled inside Taft's city limits. He was still several blocks away from the River Walk when his cell phone rang.

"Something's going on over at Landy's," said Lucas without preamble when Micah answered the phone. "Are you close?"

Micah pushed his foot down on the accelerator and flipped on his emergency blinkers. The back end of the SUV jittered around on the ice that coated the surface of the bridge as he crossed the Twilight. His heart felt as though it were leaping haphazardly all over his chest. "I'm close, but call 911 anyway, will you?"

"Already did, but the deputies are both out on accidents. Tom's off duty, but he's on his way."

"Meet you there."

Micah dropped the phone into the passenger seat, slowed down enough to look both ways and ran a red light. It figured that when he was in a life-or-death hurry, both of Taft's stoplights would be red.

"Something's going on over at Landy's."

Something. What in the hell was something?

He parked the Blazer down the street from Landy's house and sprinted at a slant across neighboring yards until he reached the River Walk behind her house. Lucas waited in the shadows.

"I was making a last round on the watch," he said softly, "and I saw movement across the river. I can't even swear that it was a person, just that something moved. The house looks fine, but Landy's phone was busy. That doesn't mean anything, of course. She could be talking or have left it off the hook. But I just didn't like it." He looked uneasy.

Micah dropped his keys, cursed, and picked them up,

searching through them until he found the one to Landy's back door. "Why don't you wait out here for Tom?" he suggested. Landy wouldn't be happy with him if he managed to get himself killed, but she'd be even less so if he took Lucas out with him.

The older man raised an eyebrow. "I don't think so."

"Damn it, Lucas, I don't want to have to worry about you if there's someone in there."

"So don't." Lucas gave him a slight push toward the door. "You worry about Landy and I'll cover your ass. I owe it to your father."

Micah felt instinctive dread coursing through him. The quiet was so unnatural, as though even the river wildlife lay still in fear.

"Will you at least give me a minute to get upstairs before you charge?"

"That I can do. I'll check the downstairs while you go up."

The house was dark and eerily silent, even though nightlights spread a ghostly glimmer through the rooms. There was a feeling of emptiness, and Micah forced back a panic born of dread. *Please.*

He made it to Landy's partially open bedroom door without making a sound, and he reflected grimly that successfully sneaking out of the house as a teenager had lasting advantages. He knew how to step where the nails were on the stairs. And he knew how to be patient, how to wait for his eyes to grow accustomed to changes in light, how to be quiet no matter what.

He flattened himself against the wall, then leaned

around the door to peer into the room. He could see Landy lying on her back in bed. She looked pale and still in the shadowy glow of the hallway nightlight.

Pale, that was, except for the blood that seemed to be spattered everywhere, making the roses on the bedding and the wallpaper into something ugly and macabre.

Patience was no longer an option.

Landy forced her eyes open.

She felt weak and disoriented, and the room seemed darker than it should have been so close to dawn. She was alone on the bed. Had he gone? Was she dead?

In slow-motion horror, she watched the door of the room open wider, making room for Micah's partially crouched form to slip inside. The increased light from the hallway allowed her to see something else.

The intruder wasn't gone, wasn't gone at all.

"Micah, he's behind the door!" She wanted to scream the words, but her voice wasn't working right and they came out in disjointed croaks. *Damn!*

As the intruder's arm rose, Landy lunged to the side of the bed, trying to ignore her wooziness and the stickiness of blood. She misjudged where the edge of the mattress was and landed on the floor on her not-quite-perfect hip with another croaking scream.

But she was able to scramble clumsily, her breath rasping, to where the hidden box was attached to the bed frame, to press the button that kept it closed, and draw the handgun from its red velvet resting place.

And, before the hand with the flashing blade in it had time to complete its downward arc toward Micah, Landy released the gun's safety and fired.

The knife dropped and so, thank God, did the intruder.

Before the revolver slipped from her hand to land on the carpet with a soft thump, she thought sadly that history truly did repeat itself.

Another person had died at her hand.

"Good grief, woman, do you think I'm made of Band-Aids and sutures or something?" Maria Simcox complained, daubing away at superficial cuts on Landy's arm. She'd already wrapped the worst of it, closing the wounds on her neck with butterfly bandages and an occasional stitch. "Couldn't you have shot him *before* he did all this?"

"You've been married to a cop too long, Maria," said Jessie, busy bandaging the other arm. "You're starting to sound like Tom."

"Well, yes, I suppose I am." Maria glared at Landy. "Because I think it's too bad you didn't kill the SOB."

"Spoken as a true preserver of human life," came her husband's dry voice from behind her. "I'm in here as a member of law enforcement," he said before Maria could round on him, "because Micah's going to tear down the waiting room if he doesn't find something out pretty soon."

"Then you'll need to restrain him, won't you?" said his wife sharply. "We're a little busy in here."

"Just tell me if she's gonna be all right," he persisted. "I should have been there before she got hurt, and I wasn't."

"She'll be fine, now get out." But her voice softened.

Landy grabbed at Maria's hand. "Where's Micah? Is he all right?"

"I'm sorry, I should have said. He's fine, out there tearing down the waiting room like Tom said."

Now that she knew Micah was safe, Landy tried to absorb the words that had seemed to fly around somewhere above her head. "Allie's husband. I didn't kill him?"

"No, honey." Maria stopped her crisp movements long enough to squeeze Landy's fingers. "But if I'd let Jessie go in the ambulance with him when they took him to the hospital at Lawrenceburg, she might have finished him off."

"Would that have been a problem?" Jessie turned her back and banged some things around.

"Not for me," said Maria cheerfully. "Am I hurting you, Landy?"

"No." But she could feel tears slipping from her eyes. "Jess? I couldn't stand it, you know, being responsible for someone else's dying."

"I know." Jessie abandoned trying to put dents in heavy-duty stainless steel equipment and mopped at Landy's tears, then at her own. "But if he hadn't been stopped, it would have been only a matter of time for Allison and maybe for the kids, too."

"Yup." Maria gave Jessie a pat on the shoulder and took Landy's hand again. "I'd say you were probably responsible for someone living."

* * *

As scars went, she had worse ones. Fractured fingers that had healed a little less than straight. Front teeth that were capped after being broken. Surgery scars that made wearing shorts an act of courage.

Compared to those, the marks on her arms and the ones on her neck weren't bad at all. For the most part, Maria said, they would go away in time.

But Jason Scott had wounded her in places even Blake Trent hadn't reached. She understood that as twisted as it was, Blake's abuse had been born from the only way he knew to love her. That comprehension had given her the ability to forgive him even though she was aware she'd never entirely forgiven herself for his death. Jason Scott had no such excuse—he was a stranger, he didn't have her sympathy, and Landy felt it difficult to accept this almost random act of violence.

She had learned to live around the fear that had become a part of her life, to laugh when she admitted to being afraid of everything. Not that it was funny, but it kept her from crying in front of people.

For a while there, she'd forgotten to be scared. She'd found freedom and joy with Micah. They'd dated and danced and made love and it had been so much fun. Happiness had slipped in and caught her unaware and when she'd noticed it, she'd thought Oh, yes, finally, and hugged it close.

And now her fear of men—all men—resurfaced.

It came to a head a few days later, when she and Micah were sitting and watching the Twilight River flow by. "I can't be with you anymore," she told Micah. "It was wrong of me to think I could have a relationship." She couldn't bear to meet his eyes.

"So we're back to that, are we?"

She flinched, then nodded reluctantly. She angled toward him on the bench where they sat, her hand shaping his jaw. "It's not you, it's me."

He turned his face into her fingers, his lips warm against her palm. "It's both of us, Lundy. You're giving up too easily."

"No." She stared at the Twilight. "The last shot's been fired and the fat lady has wailed her final lament."

Chapter Twenty

Window Over the Sink, Taft Tribune: *It's December. I wonder how many of Taft's children will soon be riding new bicycles and skateboards. Keep an eye out for them when you're traveling, won't you? We can't, of course, protect them from all harm, but we can certainly try.*

Micah knocked on Landy's back door at eight o'clock on the first Sunday morning in December.

"You got coffee?" he asked, holding up a bag of doughnuts. "Mine was so bad even I couldn't drink it. And I know we'll probably keep the rumor mill grinding if we show up at church together, but I'll risk it. How about you?"

"Me, too." The sun wasn't out, but Landy could have sworn she felt its warmth. She hadn't seen Micah all week, and now she had new regrets to linger over along with all the old ones. "Come in."

"I still have your key," he said, stepping inside. "Do you want it back?"

It had been such a big stride in the giving of her heart when she'd handed him the key—she couldn't bear the backward step of its return. "No."

At first it was awkward, sitting at right angles from each other the way they had so many times before, with her nylon-clad knee brushing his Dockers-covered one every time she moved. But, by midway through the second cup of coffee, they talked easily. Of Allie and the girls, Eli and Jessie, Ethan and Nancy. The loneliness was still there, but it was...better.

"Colby doesn't look very well," Landy said. "And his parents look exhausted."

"The cancer is more aggressive this time around," he said, sadness putting an empty place in his voice. "The only hope now is a bone marrow transplant."

They were both on the marrow donation list—Landy thought at least half the town was—but a donor hadn't been found at the time of Colby's recurrence, and it appeared the rigorous round of chemotherapy had only bought the toddler a little time.

Church was crowded, but Landy noticed that neither of Colby's parents were there. "One of them usually comes," she murmured to Micah, "even if Colby's not well."

"I know." His arm came around her and they leaned into each other a bit, worrying together for the little boy everybody loved.

But the news, when it came at the end of the service, was good. Or at least, they all prayed it was. A donor had finally been found, and Colby was in the hospital in Cincinnati. The transplant would take place the following day, but Colby was very, very ill and the procedure alone might be too much for him.

Without discussion, Micah turned in the direction of Cincinnati when they left the church parking lot. "I can help him sleep," said Micah, his voice rough. "I'll sing 'Twist and Shout' and he'll sleep just to avoid it."

She took his hand and held it.

Even after the exhausting ride to Cincinnati and back, Landy couldn't sleep. Every time she closed her eyes, Colby's smiling countenance superimposed itself on the back of her eyelids. "Snake it up, baby now!" he had bellowed in toddler-ese when they left. "Twiss and snout!" He'd given her a wet kiss on her cheek, and she'd left lipstick and a couple of wayward tears on his.

And the words of Colby's mother kept coming back: "I couldn't stand it—to have never had him, to have never known him, to have never loved him. Even if we should lose him tonight, I wouldn't—not for anything—trade one minute of the time we've had with him."

There was no rest to be had. "You're giving up too easily." Micah's voice seemed to echo through the silent empty space that was her heart. "It's both of us." He hadn't kissed her goodbye when he'd left tonight, though he'd touched her cheek in the same place as Colby's childish lips had. Like a love-struck teenager, she hadn't washed that cheek when she'd taken her shower. She'd pressed her face to her pillow when she'd gotten into bed, hoping to be able to feel his touch.

But still she couldn't sleep. The clock in the hall signaled loudly that it was three o'clock and she was still awake. She'd give it a few more minutes— time to just close her eyes and remember the warmth and the scent and the touch of Micah Walker.

She didn't know what woke her after barely two hours. Not the known yet unfamiliar sound of an intruder, not a noise at all. She felt no fear, only an odd sense of elation that fluttered inside.

"To have never had him, to have never known him, to have never loved him. Even if we should lose him tonight, I wouldn't—not for anything—trade one minute of the time we've had him."

Ten minutes later, Landy walked to Micah's house, enjoying the Christmas lights around the darkened river. Surely he would be awake. If she'd been unable to sleep, he would have been, too, wouldn't he?

"I'm up now," he said a few minutes later, pushing open the door and yawning. "Is something wrong?"

"No, but you might want to take notes, Mr. Reporter, because I only intend to say this once." She stepped inside, brushing against his bare chest—only partly on purpose—and met his gaze. "Micah, will you marry me? If it doesn't work out, if I'm still scared of every-thing, I promise I'll let you go."

The pewter-colored eyes were inscrutable. "No."

Oh, Lord, what was she supposed to say to that? Didn't he know how scary it had been to come here?

Well, it actually hadn't been scary at all; rather it had been...liberating—yes, that was it. Liberating. But what did he mean, no? "You won't?"

"Not that way." His voice lightened and warmed, and his arms slipped around her so that she had no choice but to lean right up against his hair-roughened stomach and chest. "I'll marry you, but we're not putting any limits or qualifications on it. If you're scared, we'll fix it, if you're in a shooting mood, we'll fix that, too—I'll bring you a cake in jail with a file in it or something, and I'll be waiting when you get out. Same goes for you. If I find myself up a tree, I expect you to bring a ladder and two cups of coffee and join me there."

"But—"

"No buts. It's time to bet the whole pot or get out of the casino."

She felt laughter beginning deep in her chest. "You went to the gambling boat last weekend, didn't you?"

"Sure did," he said, looking disgruntled. "Lost my whole forty dollars." He waited, and silence hummed between them. "Well, Landy, what do you say? I've got nothing else to lose. After the forty bucks, I mean."

"I don't have a new dress."

"I don't care if you don't."

"When do you want to do it?"

"How about Christmas Eve? That way, I'll always remember our anniversary."

Excitement lent an unaccustomed quiver to her voice. "You don't think people might be surprised?"

His chuckle was a caress. "Why should they be surprised? We were in church together yesterday."

Epilogue

Window Over the Sink, Taft Tribune: *My name isn't Susan Billings and I don't have any children, though I do have a nice new husband. While it's true that I have a window over my sink and it does overlook the Twilight, the life I described was only the one I wished I had. The feelings I've written about in the Window Over the Sink are all real; and I hope you've experienced the good ones with me.*

One of the biggest truths I ever wrote was in my very first column, when I said there's great comfort in being a damn fool once in a while. What I didn't say and should have was that if you don't watch what you're doing, you get way too comfortable being a damn fool. You lose yourself

*in the fear and the emptiness and the carefulness
of it. You...well, you lose yourself, that's all.*

*My name isn't Susan, it's Landy. And I'm not
going to be a fool anymore.*

Her house couldn't be a depot anymore. Eli made the
announcement on Christmas Eve, a few weeks later, as
everyone unwound after the second wedding reception
to take place in the St. John house in as many months.
And this time he meant it. While it was true that Jason
Scott was going to spend some time in prison, he wasn't
the only predator out there. Personally, Eli didn't give
a horn off Adam's ox if Landy *never* got her quilt done.

However, since Landy, the Christmas Eve bride, was
now going to live with Micah in his house, and Nancy
and Ethan were moving into Landy's house, Eli guessed
all bets were off. He also said that there was no reason
for Micah and Landy to have brand new babies of their
own when so many neighborhood children were
scarcely used. Besides, Eli and Jessie needed somewhere to leave nine of them while they went on their
honeymoon sometime in May.

"Why not borrow this one and make it ten even?"
said Landy, hitching a fast-healing Colby up onto her
hip and kissing the top of his head, where his new-
penny-red hair lay soft and curly. She grinned at Micah.
"That way, we can take our own team and a spare when
you umpire the softball and Little League games."

"And since your columnist identity isn't a secret
anymore, you can cover the games for the paper," said

Micah. He stood beside the tree in front of the windows facing the river. "Come here, Mrs. Walker."

She handed Colby off to Nancy and came and slid in under his arm. Shrieks of laughter echoed up the Twilight as the St. John and Browning children threw indiscriminate snowballs at each other and at innocent passersby. In the library, the Liars from Down at Jenny's arm wrestled and squabbled long and loud about politics. In the kitchen, Eli and Jessie argued over the value of ranch dressing versus vinegar and oil.

"The Walk used to be such a quiet place," Landy murmured, "so dignified."

"Great Noah's ark," bellowed Eli in what his children referred to as his Sermon on the Mount voice, "isn't there room on the table for both kinds?"

"More fun now, though," said Micah. He kissed Landy and yelled toward the kitchen, "All kinds, Eli. All kinds."

* * * * *

For a sneak preview of Marie Ferrarella's
DOCTOR IN THE HOUSE,
coming to NEXT in September,
please turn the page.

He didn't look like an unholy terror.

But maybe that reputation was exaggerated, Bailey DelMonico thought as she turned in her chair to look toward the doorway.

The man didn't seem scary at all.

Dr. Munro, or Ivan the Terrible, was tall, with an athletic build and wide shoulders. The cheekbones beneath what she estimated to be day-old stubble were prominent. His hair was light brown and just this side of unruly. Munro's hair looked as if he used his fingers for a comb and didn't care who knew it.

The eyes were brown, almost black as they were aimed at her. There was no other word for it. Aimed. As if he was debating whether or not to fire at point-blank range.

Somewhere in the back of her mind, a line from a B movie, "Be afraid—be very afraid…" whispered along the perimeter of her brain. Warning her. Almost against her will, it caused her to brace her shoulders. Bailey had to remind herself to breathe in and out like a normal person.

The chief of staff, Dr. Bennett, had tried his level best to put her at ease and had almost succeeded. But an air of tension had entered with Munro. She wondered if Dr. Bennett was bracing himself as well, bracing for some kind of disaster or explosion.

"Ah, here he is now," Harold Bennett announced needlessly. The smile on his lips was slightly forced, and the look in his gray, kindly eyes held a warning as he looked at his chief neurosurgeon. "We were just talking about you, Dr. Munro."

"Can't imagine why," Ivan replied dryly.

Harold cleared his throat, as if that would cover the less than friendly tone of voice Ivan had just displayed. "Dr. Munro, this is the young woman I was telling you about yesterday."

Now his eyes dissected her. Bailey felt as if she was undergoing a scalpel-less autopsy right then and there. "Ah yes, the Stanford Special."

He made her sound like something that was listed at the top of a third-rate diner menu. There was enough contempt in his voice to offend an entire delegation from the UN.

Summoning the bravado that her parents always claimed had been infused in her since the moment she first drew breath, Bailey put out her hand. "Hello. I'm Dr. Bailey DelMonico."

Ivan made no effort to take the hand offered to him. Instead, he slid his long, lanky form bonelessly into the chair beside her. He proceeded to move the chair ever so slightly so that there was even more space between them. Ivan faced the chief of staff, but the words he spoke were addressed to her.

"You're a doctor, DelMonico, when I say you're a doctor," he informed her coldly, sparing her only one frosty glance to punctuate the end of his statement.

Harold stifled a sigh. "Dr. Munro is going to take over your education. Dr. Munro—" he fixed Ivan with a steely gaze that had been known to send lesser doctors running for their antacids, but, as always, seemed to have no effect on the chief neurosurgeon "—I want you to award her every consideration. From now on, Dr. DelMonico is to be your shadow, your sponge and your assistant." He emphasized the last word as his eyes locked with Ivan's. "Do I make myself clear?"

For his part, Ivan seemed completely unfazed. He merely nodded, his eyes and expression unreadable. "Perfectly."

His hand was on the doorknob. Bailey sprang to her feet. Her chair made a scraping noise as she moved it back and then quickly joined the neurosurgeon before he could leave the office.

Closing the door behind him, Ivan leaned over and whispered into her ear, "Just so you know, I'm going to be your worst nightmare."

Bailey DelMonico has finally
gotten her life on track, and is
passionate about her recent career
change. Nothing will stand in the way
of her becoming a doctor...that is,
until she's paired with the sharp-tongued
Dr. Ivan Munro.

Watch the sparks fly in

Doctor in the House

by *USA TODAY* Bestselling Author

Marie Ferrarella

Available September 2007

Intrigued? Read more at
TheNextNovel.com

HARLEQUIN®

Next™

HN88141

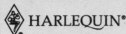

HARLEQUIN®

NExt™

GET $1.⁰⁰ OFF

your purchase of any
Harlequin NEXT novel.

Receive $1.⁰⁰ off

any Harlequin NEXT novel.

Available wherever books are sold, including most bookstores, supermarkets, drugstores and discount stores.

Coupon expires February 28, 2008.
Redeemable at participating retail outlets
in the U.S. only. Limit one coupon per customer.

5 65373 00076 2   (8100) 0 11436

HNCPNSSEUS09

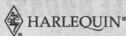 HARLEQUIN®

N$\overset{e}{x}$t™

GET $1.^{00} OFF
your purchase of any Harlequin NEXT novel.

Receive $1.^{00} off

any Harlequin NEXT novel.

Available wherever books are sold, including most bookstores, supermarkets, drugstores and discount stores.

Coupon expires February 28, 2008.
Redeemable at participating retail outlets
in Canada only. Limit one coupon per customer.

52608041

REQUEST YOUR FREE BOOKS!

2 FREE NOVELS PLUS 2 FREE GIFTS!

Ⓥ *Silhouette*®

SPECIAL EDITION®

Life, Love and Family!

YES! Please send me 2 FREE Silhouette Special Edition® novels and my 2 FREE gifts. After receiving them, if I don't wish to receive any more books, I can return the shipping statement marked "cancel." If I don't cancel, I will receive 6 brand-new novels every month and be billed just $4.24 per book in the U.S., or $4.99 per book in Canada, plus 25¢ shipping and handling per book and applicable taxes, if any*. That's a savings of at least 15% off the cover price! I understand that accepting the 2 free books and gifts places me under no obligation to buy anything. I can always return a shipment and cancel at any time. Even if I never buy another book from Silhouette, the two free books and gifts are mine to keep forever.

235 SDN EEYU   335 SDN EEY6

Name	(PLEASE PRINT)

Address	Apt.

City	State/Prov.	Zip/Postal Code

Signature (if under 18, a parent or guardian must sign)

Mail to the **Silhouette Reader Service™**:
IN U.S.A.: P.O. Box 1867, Buffalo, NY 14240-1867
IN CANADA: P.O. Box 609, Fort Erie, Ontario L2A 5X3
Not valid to current Silhouette Special Edition subscribers.

Want to try two free books from another line?
Call 1-800-873-8635 or visit www.morefreebooks.com.

* Terms and prices subject to change without notice. NY residents add applicable sales tax. Canadian residents will be charged applicable provincial taxes and GST. This offer is limited to one order per household. All orders subject to approval. Credit or debit balances in a customer's account(s) may be offset by any other outstanding balance owed by or to the customer. Please allow 4 to 6 weeks for delivery.

Your Privacy: Silhouette is committed to protecting your privacy. Our Privacy Policy is available online at www.eHarlequin.com or upon request from the Reader Service. From time to time we make our lists of customers available to reputable firms who may have a product or service of interest to you. If you would prefer we not share your name and address, please check here. ☐

SSE07

COMING NEXT MONTH